The Sweet Life

The Sweet Life

REBECCA LIM

THE HIGH STREET PUBLISHING COMPANY

The High Street Publishing Company

highstreetpublishing@gmail.com

First published in 2008 by Allen & Unwin

Copyright © Rebecca Lim 2022

All rights reserved. No part of this book may be reproduced or transmitted in any form or by any means, electronic or mechanical, including photocopying, recording or by any information storage and retrieval system, without prior permission in writing from the publisher. *The Australian Copyright Act 1968* (the Act) allows a maximum of one chapter or ten per cent of this book, whichever is the greater, to be photocopied by any educational institution for its educational purposes provided that the educational institution (or body that administers it) has given a remuneration notice to Copyright Agency Limited (cal) under the Act.

National Library of Australia Cataloguing-in-Publication entry:
Lim, Rebecca (Rebecca Pec Ca), 1972-
The sweet life

For secondary school age.

ISBN 9780645573107 (PBK)
ISBN 9780645300499 (EBK
A823.4

Cover design by Megan Ellis and Rebecca Lim
Cover photograph © Bogdan Brasoveanu (All kind of people)/Shutterstock

10 9 8 7 6 5 4 3

To Leni, with love always

Janey

For as long as Janey could remember, it had just been her and her mum.

They'd been a unit. A force to be reckoned with, the Gordon Girls. Best friends. And now her mum was gone and only Janey was left.

Everything was a nightmare. She felt as though the sound had been turned down on her world, with all the colour and joy drained out of it. Like she was moving alone through a fog, with everyone else going at normal speed around her. Janey just couldn't fathom a world without her mum in it.

Mourners filed past Janey in the chapel foyer, murmuring their sympathies. The church had been packed. People had laughed and cried at the songs and stories Janey's mum had chosen for her own service. She had so many friends.

'Friends are so important,' she would always tell Janey

fiercely. 'You can't *ever* pick your family, sweetheart. But you *can* pick your friends. And the best ones will see you through anything.'

Janey had taken that advice to heart. Her best friends, Em, Gabs and Ness, were as different as night and day, but they were like her sisters. Emily Clough was petite, quiet, dark-haired and dark-eyed, and passionate about everything to do with film and theatre. One day, she wanted to be a famous director. Gabriela Epstein was a curvy, red-haired siren with an awesome singing voice and the ability to strike up a funny conversation with just about anyone. A life skill Janey wished she had. And Vanessa McAdams? She was the gorgeous, fashion-mad clothes horse of the group who worked part-time after school just to afford the latest everything. If a trend changed anywhere, she was onto it.

Which left Janey. The tall, slightly plain, very practical one with unruly red-gold shoulder-length hair and an uncontrollable case of freckles. She didn't think she was good at anything in particular, but the others always seemed to turn to her for advice, as well as the best minestrone soup in the universe.

Her three best friends stood by discreetly now, as Janey shook the hands of people she'd never met before and would probably never see again.

When it was all over and the chapel was empty, Emily and Ness each put an arm around Janey's shoulders while Gabs led the way from the silent building.

'I don't know what I should be feeling,' Janey said tearfully.

'I always thought she'd beat it, you know? She could do anything, my mum. She was a superhero.'

It was kind of true. Janey's mum, Lydia, had fallen pregnant at sixteen – the same age Janey was now – and instead of giving in to intense pressure to get rid of the baby, she'd cut off all ties with her ultra-conservative parents, moved states, lied about her age to get work, *and* kept her baby. Her boyfriend had been seventeen and never wanted to be in the picture. All her life, Janey's mum had worked hard to make sure that Janey never felt like she was missing anything. And she hadn't.

'I would *never* have had the guts to do what your mum did,' agreed Emily huskily. 'Going it alone like that. She was the strongest person I've ever met. I thought she'd beat it too.'

Ness nodded, tears welling in her eyes. They all loved Lydia Gordon, with her funky dress sense, her fantastic cooking, and her enormous laugh. It didn't feel quite *real* that she developed leukaemia so quickly and was gone in a matter of a few short months. She was so young.

'The hardest part's coming up,' replied Janey with a catch in her voice. 'You sure you guys want to come? I might lose it totally.' So far, she'd held herself together pretty well but she was thankful her mum had asked to be laid to rest privately, just the same.

Her friends nodded. 'We're with you all the way, Janes,' Gabs said. 'It can't be any worse than what you've been through already. *Come on.* She wouldn't have wanted you to be sad. There's no more pain where she is.'

To match Janey's mood, rain began to stream down out of the sky as she and her best friends and their parents climbed into the waiting hearses.

Janey sat cross-legged on her mother's bedroom floor in the fading light of late afternoon.

She'd spent the whole Saturday going through Lydia's papers, alternately laughing and crying at the crazy things her mum had thought important to keep. The house seemed so cold and unfamiliar without the smell of Lydia's favourite sandalwood incense burning, or the sound of classical music playing low somewhere in the house.

She stared at the letter she held in her hand in disbelief. It was over three years old, headed with the name of some crusty law firm in Sydney, together with the ominous words *Private and Confidential*.

Janey read the letter through several times. The words made absolutely no sense to her numb brain.

Dear Ms Gordon,

We are writing to determine whether you are the same Lydia Cromwell Gordon, birth date 9 January 1975, formerly of 'Clewes House', 18 Berkeley Crescent, Double Bay, New South Wales 2028. A family member wishes to make contact in regard to a matter that may benefit you materially. Please contact the writer on the direct line below to discuss the necessary proof of identification and to arrange contact.

That was pretty much all the letter said. But it was the words *family member* that made Janey's mind reel, because Lydia had told her several years before that Janey's grandparents had died in a car accident. Lydia had seen an article about it in the newspaper the day after it had happened, and although her eyes had been sad, her voice was hard.

'They were most likely on their way back from the country house in the Hunter Valley,' she'd said in a detached monotone, chopping vegetables furiously. 'Seems they collided with a fruit truck. Dad would've hated that. He hated mess. That's that then. We're the only Gordons left now.'

Janey had seen her mum furtively wipe away a few tears, blaming them on the onions, before she changed the subject altogether.

And now there was this letter. Lydia must never have replied, because there was no further correspondence from the law firm anywhere in her papers.

Janey got up slowly – eyes red and head thumping from a headache that had been building all afternoon – and went down the hall to the poky study where the computer lived. She fired up the internet and typed in the name of the law firm.

Her skin prickled when the search results showed that the firm still existed. And not only that, it was still at the same address. She looked up the author of the letter on the firm's website and found that he was still there too, contactable on the same number.

Janey didn't know much about her mum's life before she'd been, well, her mum. All she knew was that Lydia Gordon had been the pampered only child of wealthy, rather elderly parents who had turned on her when she wanted to keep her baby. The address mentioned in the letter meant nothing to Janey, although the birth date listed there was as familiar to her as her own. And Lydia's middle name *was* 'Cromwell', after some long-dead relative.

With a weird fluttery feeling in the pit of her stomach, Janey rubbed her eyes with the back of one hand, and created a new document. She began typing 'Dear Sir...'

Janey didn't hear back for weeks. And in those weeks her life changed radically.

Their narrow old weatherboard house was up for sale; it didn't really feel like home anymore, without her mum there. Everything that hadn't been given away in accordance with Lydia's wishes had been packed up and put into temporary storage. Janey had moved in with Gabs's family, the Epsteins, while she waited for the sale to go through. Mr Epstein was helping finalise the gazillion things that have to happen after a person dies that no sixteen-year-old is supposed to know about.

Before Lydia Gordon's illness had really taken hold, she had asked Gabs's dad to be Janey's legal guardian until she turned eighteen. But Janey wouldn't be living with the

Epsteins permanently. The sale of the house would mean a new apartment for Janey one day, and maybe enough money to live on until she finished school and decided what she wanted to do with her life.

Still, for Janey, it was a heartbreaking time. Though she was looking forward to having her own place some day, she knew she would give it all up in a heartbeat to have her mum back again.

She forgot all about the letter until a buff-coloured envelope arrived in the mail weeks later, headed with the name of the Sydney law firm in a very important-looking font.

It was Friday afternoon. Ness and Em were staying over at the Epsteins that weekend as well, and all four girls were looking forward to a long, lazy Saturday of shopping, eating and catching up on the hottest music and movies. They were poring over the latest copy of their favourite magazine together and nominating the must-haves of the new season, when Gabs's mum passed through the kitchen and slid an envelope across the island bench towards Janey.

Everyone caught sight of the envelope and began talking at once.

'Is that what I think it is?' Emily demanded. Janey had told her friends about the mysterious letter, and how she'd just sent back a reply over three years later.

'You could be the heiress to a fabulous fortune!' squealed Ness. 'And up to the eyeballs in Jimmy Choo shoes by this time next week! We could give your wardrobe a complete overhaul!'

Janey laughed as she shook her head. 'The "family member" probably got all the loot! Though goodness knows who *that* is. Even if I do give the "necessary proof of identification", someone's probably just feeling guilty about the way Mum was hounded out of home. If I'm lucky, I'll get a commemorative ashtray or something, with the family crest on it.'

'Just open it before I die of curiosity!' Gabs pleaded, handing Janey a letter opener.

Janey's hands were shaking a little as she opened the envelope and unfolded the single sheet of paper inside. She scanned it quickly, unable to keep the disappointment out of her voice. 'More hurdles.'

She blinked, a telltale sheen in her eyes. 'The lawyer says I need to provide a photo of my mum around the time I was born, and a recent photo of me. The "family member" is probably a suspicious old crone, three times removed, who wants to make sure I have the family nose.'

Her friends crowded around to read the brief, businesslike letter, which gave absolutely nothing away.

'Look on the bright side,' said Gabs. 'We just got our school photos done and you look almost decent, for a change!'

Janey took a swipe at her friend's head with a towel as the four girls headed to the outside spa.

A few days later, Janey posted the requested photos and put the whole thing out of her mind.

It was the last week of term and Janey and Gabs were running late for school again, having fought the usual battle with their hair straighteners.

'There's a letter for you,' said Gabs as she flicked through the morning mail over her breakfast cereal. 'Whoo-hoo! It's got an *Italian* postmark.'

Janey frowned as she looked at the envelope. 'Must have the wrong Jane Gordon. This letter's from a Celia Albright at the Australian embassy in Rome. I've never even left the country.'

She didn't need to say more. Unlike her besties, Janey had never had enough money to spend on the latest cute fashion buys, let alone a holiday overseas.

She ripped open the envelope and almost choked as something slipped out of the folds of the letter and splashed into her muesli.

It was a photo.

Of Janey.

As an *older* woman.

Same freckles, same angular features, same fly-away, red-gold wavy shoulder-length hair.

Janey and her mum shared the same distinctive colouring, but while Lydia had been a stunning beauty, the woman in the photo, whoever she was, was only vaguely pretty, like Janey.

'What on earth?!' Janey exclaimed, holding up the photo to show Gabs's family, who were all standing around the kitchen eating their breakfast as fast as their stomachs could stand it.

'Is that you?' said Gabs, wrinkling her nose. 'Because if it is, it must be some kind of joke. You look about forty!'

'What does the letter say, Janey?' asked Mrs Epstein cautiously.

'Yeah, read it!' Gabs's younger brother added through a mouthful of toast.

Janey unfolded the closely typed, single-page letter and began to read out loud.

> Dear Jane. Or may I call you Janey?
> No doubt you are as surprised by the enclosed photo of me as I was on receiving the photo of you.

'This is making no sense at all,' Janey muttered, studying the woman's photo again.

'Keep reading,' Mr Epstein urged. Everyone was so intrigued they'd stopped eating and forgotten all about the time.

> I'm devastated that this finds you too late for me to have met your mother, Lydia. I don't quite know what to feel. Delighted to have found you at last, but angry? sad? bitter? to have missed out on meeting the Gordons' lost daughter. Because, you see, I was one too. And would happily have stayed that way, until your grandparents used a private investigator to track me down when they realised exactly how stubborn your mother was, and that she was never coming back.

Janey grinned mistily and continued reading.

> Your grandparents were proud and difficult people. They refused to acknowledge their mistakes. But like you, I was a mistake, if you don't mind me calling you that. I was their mistake, twelve years before Lydia was born and while your grandfather was still married to someone else.

Janey gasped as the implications sank in. 'Those old hypocrites!' she said, taking a steadying breath.

> They couldn't find her, but they found me. And they left me all their money, did you know that? Because they had no one left to give it to.

Astonished, Gabs and Janey stared at each other for a moment before Janey read on.

> I should very much like to get to know you and would like to invite you to spend your upcoming school holidays with me in Rome. My daughter, Freddy (Federica), is almost your age and would love to meet her new cousin. All my details are below, and a call to the Department of Foreign Affairs should establish my credentials to your guardian's satisfaction.

Janey looked quickly across the table at Mr Epstein. He nodded. 'Shouldn't be too hard to prove if this Celia Albright is the genuine article.'

> What a mess this all is, but ultimately a happy one. Call me on the number below? I'll arrange everything, of course.
> Yours in anticipation, your aunt (!),
> Celia Albright.

Everybody was silent for a long moment before Janey said tearfully, 'Mum would've loved a trip to Rome. Rome! Imagine that.' It seemed as faraway and exotic as the moon.

'Do you think she knew?' Gabs asked, handing Janey a tissue. 'About Celia, and all that?'

Janey shook her head. 'I doubt it. But it wouldn't have changed anything. She would never have agreed to give me away, like my grandmother must have given Celia away. Like, like . . . a parcel. Isn't it funny how things turn out?'

'Right,' Mr Epstein interrupted, 'the sooner I get you lot off my hands, the sooner I can start making some calls on Janey's behalf. We've got a Roman holiday to organise, girls.'

'Wait till you tell the others!' said Gabs as she and Janey scraped their chairs back and headed for the door.

Fellini

Janey Gordon was one of those girls who everyone just *liked*.

She wasn't particularly good at sport, or one of the beautiful crowd, or even the slightest bit musical, but she was just *nice*. After spending time with Janey Gordon, most people felt better about life, the universe and everything. She had a gentle way of listening and talking things through that made a whole lot of sense. So when word got around Selbourne High that Janey was looking down the barrel of an all-expenses-paid trip to Rome, everyone was genuinely happy for her, especially after the year she'd had. All year, people had discreetly looked the other way when the strain of her mum's illness had caused her to have the occasional minor meltdown.

Within a few hours, Gabs's dad had verified Celia Albright's identity and position as Second Secretary at the Australian

Embassy in Rome. Arrangements were made for Janey to make her first ever overseas trip, fully paid for by her new aunt. Mr Epstein had also told Janey that she'd have a debit card linked to the modest sum of money her mum had left her. He lectured her about sticking to a budget and not blowing the entire amount on a two-week holiday. Janey's eyes had filled as she nodded, knowing how hard her mum had worked to save that money.

'I'm *sooooo* jealous!' said Em over lunch on the second-last day of term. 'Italy's totally the land of *La Dolce Vita*, Janes. Long lunches, fabulous coffee, gorgeous monuments, even more gorgeous guys. I can't believe you're getting a second summer in the Eternal City while we suffer through a boring winter without you! *And* your minestrone. It's too cruel.'

'*La Dolce* what?' Janey wrinkled her freckly nose.

'The Sweet Life,' said Em. 'It's, like, only the most famous film Federico Fellini – just about Italy's most famous film director – ever made. *And* it's set in Rome. I can't believe you haven't heard of it. Fellini practically invented the word *paparazzi*. Watch it before you go, you philistine.'

'Never heard of him, Em, you know-it-all,' Ness interrupted. 'Now on to more important things, Janey. Like getting you holiday-ready and fabulous before you leave. My place, after school, no excuses. I've got some looks for you to try out.'

Janey and Ness were both tall and willowy, with legs to die for. And there the similarity ended – Ness was a green-eyed blonde stunner and styling genius, who looked a million bucks on a teeny budget, while Janey was, well, just Janey. She always looked perfectly okay in her hoodies, jeans and high-tops. But it was generally acknowledged that Janey Gordon, with her cloud of untamable, fluffy red-gold hair and habit of tripping over her own size ten feet, would never set the fashion world on fire. Plus, Ness ate like a sparrow, while saying that Janey *loved* her food was a massive understatement.

Gabs rolled her eyes and groaned. 'You and your *looks*, Vanessa McAdams! Like that time you said green glitter eye shadow, an oversized cable sweater and black leggings were a really good match for someone with my hair and build!'

'And the time you insisted I buy that atrocious silver tulip-skirted bandeau dress that made me look ten times shorter than I already am,' snorted Em. 'I looked like a flowerpot man, only upside down.'

'You both looked perfectly on trend!' exclaimed Ness in hurt tones.

Her three friends giggled.

'Yeah, for someone built like Kate Moss!' said Gabs. 'Whereas *I* am built along more *Roman* lines.'

'Which brings us back to the urgent issue of your holiday wardrobe,' said Ness, turning to Janey. 'I've always said that you'd knock 'em dead if you'd just let me style you!'

Janey sighed. Usually she just zoned out when Ness launched into the subject of fashion, but for some strange reason it was suddenly really important to her that she make a good impression on her new aunt and cousin. She wanted to fly the flag for her beautiful mum, Lydia, and if that meant a bit of fashion torture, well, maybe it was worth it. Just this once.

'I don't even wear make-up, Ness,' she said. 'Never got the hang of it. And I just can't speak that whole flash-fash lingo of yours. Let's face it, I've got *zero* girly style.'

'You've got really good skin,' Ness replied.

Janey looked dubious.

'Seriously! And you should never underestimate a good foundation and concealer,' Ness continued. 'Just add a great smoky eye and nude lip and that's all you need on the make-up front. Which just leaves you to pull together some resort-worthy looks from the clothes I've picked out for you to wear. I can fix the girly style thing. It's a no-brainer.'

Ness was so good at styling herself that older girls often stopped her in the street to ask where she bought her clothes. She could make vintage look amazing. She also made stuff from scratch that looked totally couture and mixed it all up like a pro. The Olsen twins had nothing on Ness, who worked three jobs, two of which were fashion-related. Ness almost never needed to actually sell anything to anyone, because as soon as a customer clapped eyes on what Ness was wearing, they wanted it too.

'Go on, Janes,' said Em. 'Saves you worrying about what to pack. Ness has clothes to burn. She's not going to miss a suitcase full of stuff for a couple of weeks. Let her help.'

'Yeah,' Gabs agreed. 'If I could fit into Ness's stuff I'd be raiding her wardrobe every spare minute. You've never let her work her magic on you – just let her try. If you end up looking like a Roman urn or a flowerpot man, Em and I will let you know – have no fear.'

Janey found herself nodding. As the bell rang, the four girls agreed to meet up at Ness's house after school.

'I'll bring the eats,' Em volunteered, as she melted into the post-lunch corridor crowd with a wave.

Ness's room was dominated by an awesome walk-in wardrobe filled to the colour-coded brim with clothes, handbags, accessories and shoes.

Vintage was mixed in with hand-me-down high-end stuff from Ness's equally gorgeous mum, Lou Lou. One-off creations by Ness herself were rounded out with trash-fash cheapie buys that could be loved to death for one season, then thrown away. Her room was a fashionista's paradise. The only thing was, Janey and Em weren't fashionistas in the slightest, and Gabs had long ago acknowledged that she'd have to stop eating altogether to fit into any of Ness's clothes. And she wasn't about to do *that*.

'I just love food too much,' said Gabs, looking around the room longingly.

'And so you should,' Em replied. 'Have a chip.'

Gabs and Janey helped themselves to Em's stash of chilli-flavoured corn chips and sprawled across the end of Ness's double bed. Fashion magazines littered almost every surface of the bedroom. Ness was also a cosmetics junkie. Lipstick and nail polish in every conceivable shade were lined up in neat rows across her French provincial-style dressing table.

'Uh, bring it on,' Janey said warily.

'Oh no you don't, Jane Gordon. You're the house model for today, so get in there and try on outfit number one.' Ness pointed a perfectly painted fingernail – Chanel Le Vernis in Vamp, naturally – at her overflowing, room-sized walk-in robe.

Janey mooched in. 'I don't even know where my head is supposed to go,' she said a minute later, sounding muffled. 'I think my earring's caught. *Help*.'

Ness shot Em and Gabs an expressive eyebrow and marched in. A moment later, Janey emerged in a figure-skimming red-and-white striped halter-neck top over a pair of indigo jeans of the perfect degree of skinniness.

Gabs and Em gasped. The shade of red in the top shouldn't have worked with Janey's bright hair, but somehow it did.

'You look *fantastic*!' said Em. 'You've got a shape at last!'

Janey looked sheepish. 'I feel half-dressed. And I'm cold.'

'It's high summer over there, stupid,' Ness replied. 'I checked the weather channel. Now get in there and slide on look number two.'

Look number two was a vintage Diane von Furstenberg wrap dress in graphic black and white, with red platform wedges. Luckily, Ness's feet were as huge as Janey's.

'You've got *curves*, Jane Gordon,' Gabs crowed as Janey leant slinkily against the doorframe, batting her eyelashes. Her friends broke out laughing.

'Fab dress courtesy of Lou Lou's last wardrobe cleanout,' said Ness happily. 'Haven't worn it myself yet! There are at least five other outfit changes in there, Janes, so get cracking. We've got other fish to fry.'

Next, Janey appeared in a pair of denim sailor pants with heavy brass buttons, a navy-and-white striped top with three-quarter sleeves, and a pair of round-toed ballet flats.

Gabs nodded as she nibbled on a rice cracker. 'I like it. Very Gwen Stefani-esque.'

'Classic,' Em agreed. 'Very French New Wave cinema.'

The fourth of Ness's looks was a fitted orange singlet top and a black, mid-calf tulle skirt.

'Kooky combo,' said Ness as Janey pirouetted around the bedroom with her arms in the air. 'But it works, don't you think?'

Emily and Gabs nodded, in awe of Ness's fashion genius.

Further outfit changes yielded white short shorts, a silky peasant blouse in a vibrant flower print with cap sleeves and a gathered yoke, a belted grey jersey T-shirt dress, and a vintage black shift dress with bronze beading around the neckline.

'Magnifique!' Em declared, clapping as the run of outfits ended.

'*Magnifico*, you clueless wonder,' Gabs corrected. 'She's going to *Italy*, remember? Though she wouldn't look out of place in Paris. Every look a bona fide winner, Janey. If you don't come back engaged to a handsome young Italian aristocrat, I'll eat Ness's entire collection of rhinestone hairclips.'

'Deal,' said Ness. 'I was getting sick of them anyway.' She turned to Janey. 'You like?'

Janey, still in the beaded black dress, threw her hands up

in the air. 'I *like*. You were right, Ness, I needed help. I don't own anything half as glam as these. And everything works back together. Mixing and matching shouldn't be too much of a stretch for a fashion cretin like me.'

'*And* I've got the perfect suitcase for all this to go into,' Ness added. 'Genuine Anya Hindmarch, *if* you don't mind. Another Lou Lou cast-off. Covered in signature bows with a telescoping handle to save your dainty back. Wait one minute while I throw everything into it.'

Janey changed out of the dramatic black dress and reappeared in her usual striped hoodie and jeans. Gabs handed her a piece of caramel slice, which Janey devoured gratefully.

'Don't get too comfortable!' Ness said as she wheeled out the little suitcase, leaving it by her bedroom door. 'That was only the start of your kick-butt makeover. Now for a lesson in the art of cosmeceutical enhancement. Eyebrows first, I should think. They're looking a bit straggly.'

Janey groaned. 'You mean there's *more*?'

Ness dragged her over to the dressing table and began picking out bottles, tubes and brushes. Em and Gabs each popped open a can of cola, toasted one other, and settled in for the show.

Janey was so hopeless at applying eyeliner and mascara that they all ended up staying for dinner at Ness's place.

'You looked less like Janey and more like a raccoon,' mused Em as she practically inhaled Lou Lou's apricot chicken.

'No,' said Gabs cheerfully, 'like a runny panda. Tragic.'

Janey flushed. 'I told you I was no good at this stuff.'

'Not to worry, dear,' said Lou Lou, taking a sip of her wine, 'I was completely clueless about make-up at high school. And look at me now!'

Janey shot Lou Lou – who looked like a model – a look of disbelief.

'No really, I was.' Lou Lou laughed. '*And* I had a poodle perm with a sheepdog fringe, to make matters worse.'

'She's not joking,' grinned Ness's dad. 'Back when we first met, Lou Lou's look could best be described as, uh... colour blind. Luckily I saw beyond the daggy façade to the beauty within.'

Lou Lou giggled. 'Nothing matched.'

'*And* you couldn't see where you were going.'

'They can go on like this for hours,' Ness snorted. 'What they're trying to say is that there's hope for you yet, Janey.'

'On an entirely different topic,' said Em, pushing away her empty plate, 'did you get many comments on MySpace about your trip to Rome?'

Janey nodded. 'So many that I haven't had time to work my way through them all! If it's okay, Gabs, I'm going to log a couple of extra hours on your computer tonight. I know it's still technically a school night but I want to touch base with as many people as possible before I leave for Rome. Aunt Celia's probably got a computer I can use, but if she doesn't, I don't want to leave my fans hanging!'

Her friends laughed. But actually it wasn't far from the

truth. Janey had a humungous number of online buddies because her About Me blurb was so laugh-out-loud funny and so utterly Janey that she'd attracted quite a fan base. She would proclaim proudly, 'My mum is my hero!' and wasn't afraid to say other daggy stuff that people were thinking, but were too afraid to post themselves: 'I *hate it* when people are mad at me' and 'I love the smell of the garden after it rains' and 'I'm really shy till I get to know you, so keep on trying! I'm worth it!' Online, Janey was a lot bolder than she was in person, and her personality really shone through.

Her photo was cute too, because Ness had caught her smiling in the sunshine when she hadn't known a camera was focused on her. The natural-looking photo was a refreshing change from all the seedy prom queen photos that were out there. It was obvious she was the real deal, and not a try-hard, fake friend collector.

'Sure thing, Janes,' said Gabs, polishing off the last of her chicken.

'Better get you girls home then,' said Mr McAdams. 'Don't want to keep those fans waiting!'

It was almost midnight. Gabs had long since begged Janey to stop reading to her from her MySpace page and had gone to sleep. Like the good friend she was, Janey was replying to as many comments as she could and was having about a dozen simultaneous conversations with friends who were currently online, most of whom she'd never met in real life.

She was about to log out when a new message came through from Razzle Girl.

 Hey chickie, who's this Fellini dude? Sounds heavy. *Razzle Girl*

Janey frowned into the computer screen.

 Wat? Don't know no Fellini. *x X Janey G X x*

Where had she heard that name before? *Fellini*. It came to her a moment later. Em's genius (but dead) Italian film director.

What an odd coincidence, she thought. She didn't remember accepting 'Fellini' as a friend, but with new friends coming on board all the time, she probably had.

 C ur page, Id read if I were u. Sounds serious. Creepy even. *Razzle Girl*

Janey hastily closed out of about a million other windows and scrolled further up her own comments list, which she'd been tackling from the bottom. She realised with a sinking feeling that she still had dozens of comments to read and reply to. An absolute avalanche of excited mail had arrived after her last blog about her upcoming trip. But with the last day of term still to get through, she needed to hit the sack *now*, or she'd be a bona fide zombie in the morning.

I'll just check out this Fellini guy's comment, she thought to herself, searching up through the most current comments until she found him. It had been posted on the same day she'd uploaded her latest blog.

Rather than using a personal photo like almost all of Janey's 369 online friends, Fellini was represented by a photo of a serious car wreck. It was a shiny black sedan with a smashed-in bonnet. The wreck was surrounded by pieces of glass and twisted metal. Janey went cold as she peered more closely at the photo. She thought she could make out a person slumped against the steering wheel which, like all European cars, was a right-hand drive.

The message beside the chilling image made Janey recoil.

Hey this could happen to u. In Rome.

Fellini

Janey frantically scrolled up the remaining comments on her page with shaking fingers and found one further message.

Don't go. Or bad things will go down.
You heard it here first.   *Fellini*

Her insides went ice cold.

I would've remembered an avatar like that! she thought. *The guy must've changed it recently.*

Skin crawling, Janey clicked on Fellini's profile. All it said was that 'Fellini' was male, twenty-one and Italian, and had logged in as recently as today. His page was largely blank, as he had no blogs, blurbs or other photos posted. Which said exactly *zero* about him. Scanning the rest of his meagre page, she saw that the guy had just one friend and that one friend was . . . *her*.

Janey quickly logged out, telling herself it was just sour grapes from some jealous creepazoid who'd browsed her at random and was in the mood for causing trouble.

Still, sleep was a long time coming that night.

Luca

She flew for twenty-six bewildering hours to emerge into the chaos that was Rome's Leonardo da Vinci airport at six in the morning.

There were people everywhere: shouting, sweating, cursing and pushing their way up ragged, haphazard queues to reach customs windows that were closed, then suddenly opened, then closed again. And when they all cleared customs, there was more shouting, sweating and cursing when people discovered that several flights' worth of baggage had somehow been mixed up and was now piled at random throughout the arrival hall in every available nook and cranny.

But Janey didn't mind because Janey was in Rome. *Rome*! And Lou Lou's lovely suitcase was the easiest bag to spot. And even though her hair was frizzy and her nose was shiny, everything was all right with her world because she still looked cool and classy in her denim sailor pants and jaunty French top and – as soon as she walked through the sliding doors into the golden heat of a Roman morning – *the most beautiful young man she had ever seen in her life* was standing on the footpath, holding up a sign with *her* name on it.

If she'd been the swooning type, she would have, because the stranger held out a strong, tanned hand to her and said in a deliciously husky voice: 'Buongiorno, signorina Gordon. I would know you anywhere. I am Luca Sarti.'

Luca was tall, olive-skinned and clean-shaven, with dark curling hair and dark smiling eyes. His brilliant white teeth were ever-so-slightly crooked and he had a dimple in his right cheek. He was wearing a killer black suit, a crisp white shirt and a textured silvery-grey tie. He didn't appear to be much older than she was. To Janey, he looked utterly perfect.

Speechless, Janey did a panicky sort of half-nod, half-smile thing and let Luca take the handle of her suitcase. Not stopping to question why someone who looked like Luca would know someone who looked like her *anywhere*, she floated along beside him wordlessly until she caught sight of the car he was leading her towards.

Like all European cars, it was black and shiny and right-hand drive. It also looked very much like the smashed-up sedan in Fellini's MySpace avatar. Except not smashed up. Yet.

Janey stopped dead in her tracks.

'Is something the matter, signorina?' Luca said with some concern as he caught sight of Janey's frozen expression.

'Um, w-who sent you?' she stammered. 'And where was

it that you're supposed to be, uh, taking me?' She had to ask. The coincidence was too weird.

His brow cleared. 'Of course! It is wise of you to make the question. I am driver for the Australian embassy. Celia Albright, she send me. She make the apology, but she has the urgent meeting. To do with the trade. Così – it is just I, Luca.'

Janey's smile returned – though her heart was still thundering a little – which in turn made Luca smile.

'It is okay now, to go?' he asked, gesturing at the car.

'It is very, um, okay,' Janey replied with a grin that lit up her features.

Luca went to open the back door to allow Janey to sit in solitary splendour like a visiting head of state. 'Oh, I'd much rather sit next to you,' she said shyly. 'If that's okay. Then you can tell me about all the places we're passing so that I'll remember everything exactly the way I saw it and be able to tell my friends.'

'You 'ave never been to Roma?' Luca asked with surprise as he clicked the boot shut and returned to open the front passenger door for her. Janey could tell from his expression that she was not his usual type of sophisticated passenger.

Janey shook her head. 'I've never been anywhere. This is the first time I've ever been out of Australia. So I want to drink it all in, every last tree, building and, uh, traffic island.'

She felt her face flush an awful beetroot red. *If that didn't sound kooky and weird*, she thought, wishing her stupid tongue would fall out, *then nothing would*.

Luca just smiled. 'Bene!' he said as he dropped into the seat beside her and slid on his rock-and-roll blue-tinted aviators. 'Then we will take the long way, no? And I will show you the places per i turisti *and* the secret places – where to get the good coffee, the gelato and the pasticcerie . . .'

And with that, Luca slid the large black car into gear and they were gunning down the motorway into Rome at a speed that took Janey's breath away.

Luca was even better than his word.

As promised, he drove her past all the usual places, like the Colosseum and the Vatican, pointing out the smart shopping streets and telling her the best times to visit the crazy tourist haunts like Trevi Fountain and the Pantheon. But he also showed her the tiny side street that would take her to a shop that sold only toys made out of wood, and the store that made the most beautiful writing paper she'd ever seen. And not only that, he threw the car into a ridiculously tiny, totally illegal parking spot and took her down a winding cobbled lane that led to the best coffee in Rome made by the barista with the most attitude in Rome and bought her a macchiato ('It is the only way to drink the coffee, signorina'). Then he urged her back into the car and whisked her up and down narrow laneways to point out the places where the gelato, pasta or pizza was good enough to cross town for, where to buy the best leather gloves in the world, the most high-fashion shoes for not-so-high-fashion prices.

'Because I know about the women and the shoes,' he said knowingly, which made Janey's heart lurch in her chest as she wondered whether he had a girlfriend and how old he was, and how she was so not his type that she shouldn't even be wondering about stupid stuff like that.

And then Luca double-parked outside an alimentari – or grocery shop – and conjured up a delicious lunch of things she'd never tried before: panino with bresaola and bocconcini, topped with a simple rocket and tomato salad, with takeaway cups of freshly squeezed lemon juice over ice. They ate perched on the side of a tumbling renaissance fountain beneath shady trees in the gardens of the glorious Villa Borghese, and it felt to Janey as though she'd known Luca forever.

Usually she was a tongue-tied, blushing mess when it came to meeting boys, but somehow she found herself really *talking* to Luca. She even stopped stammering! It was a miracle. Janey told him all about her mum, her friends, herself and what she hoped for one day.

'Em is a total movie buff,' Janey said between sips of her deliciously sour drink. 'She knows every frame of *La Dolce Vita* like she shot it, instead of Fellini, and she can't believe I'm *here* and *she's* back in Australia trying to stay warm.'

For a second, Janey recalled the Fellini she'd met online, and she shot Luca a quick sidelong look. But nothing in the guy's expression had changed at the mention of the famous director's name. He just continued to look drop-dead gorgeous and, amazingly, interested in what she was saying. Janey relaxed a little more.

'My other friend, Gabs, is a diva in waiting. The *good* kind! She has the biggest, brassiest singing voice you've ever heard. I really think she'll be world famous one day. And she's so warm, and so – oh, I don't know – *including*, that when she talks to you, it's like she's reached out and given you a hug. While Ness is just stunning. Blonde, tall, lean, beautiful inside and out, and she's got the greenest green cat's eyes you've ever seen and is so nice that she lent me all the clothes I'm wearing...'

Janey stopped speaking and blushed. *Now I'm going to sound like a complete idiot who can't even dress herself.* She self-consciously tucked a stray strand of wavy hair behind one ear.

'You are lucky to have such friends! It says much about you,' said Luca, which was the perfect thing to say and put Janey so much at ease that when Luca's mobile phone rang and he commenced to bark into it in clipped Italian, she realised that it was now way past noon and Luca had a job to return to.

He flipped his mobile shut.

'Mi dispiace,' he said regretfully, 'but I am shortly expected at the Ministero della Difesa Aeronautica and I will be late if we do not go now.'

Luca guided Janey out of the gardens and back to the car. A moment later he was navigating the crazy traffic on the Corso Italia as though he had a death wish.

He saw Janey clutch the edges of her seat from the corner of his eye and laughed out loud.

'What can I say?' he shrugged as he slid his sunglasses

back on and overtook two speeding trucks and a merging van. 'It is Italy, it is the way we drive, the way we are.'

Janey smiled back weakly and wished the road to Celia's place would last forever, even if she wasn't sure she'd make it there in one piece.

A short time later, Luca guided the black car into an impossibly tight parking spot in front of an elegant 1920s villa that housed some of the senior staff of the Australian Embassy. The villa was in a graceful suburb located just north of the towering ancient city walls that surround the historical centre of Rome and its legendary seven hills.

'We are here,' Luca said, releasing Janey's seatbelt with a flourish. He sprang out of the car and opened her door. 'Signora Albright and her daughter occupy Appartamento 2C. You ascend there, and then press the security, you understand?'

Janey nodded. 'Well, goodbye, and, um, thank you,' she said, wondering whether she'd ever see him again.

Luca, already on his mobile speaking Italian to somebody else, retrieved Janey's suitcase and placed the handle in her hand.

It had to be a woman, thought Janey with a twinge as Luca jumped back into the car, still talking and smiling, *to have him looking like that.*

With a last wave that she wasn't sure he'd even registered, Janey paused beneath the grand front portico of the villa, her heart in her mouth as she watched Luca's death-defying u-turn.

He's total heart attack material, she thought. *But in* such *a good way.*

The entrance to the villa was blocked by wrought iron security doors that were at least three metres high. Janey scanned the keypad on the wall and pressed the button for 2C.

'Pronto?' purred a young female voice over the intercom.

Janey wondered if she had arrived at the right place. 'I'm sorry,' she apologised. 'I'm looking for Celia Albright.' She suddenly realised how tired she was. Being with Luca had masked it, but now it seemed almost too much of an effort to stand upright.

There was a long pause, during which Janey thought the girl might have hung up or walked away.

'Oh, it's you,' the voice finally drawled through the speaker in lightly accented English. 'You're *late.*'

The security doors clicked open, and Janey found herself standing in front of the kind of black, wrought iron, vintage cage lift that she'd only seen in movies starring Audrey Hepburn.

She pressed the button for the second floor. The villa had three floors with several apartments on each one. As the lift ascended, Janey glimpsed the first landing through the bars of the lift. It was decorated in subtle shades of cream, muted green and gold, with tasteful urns, paintings and antiques placed about the communal hallway.

As the lift doors opened onto the second floor, Janey found herself face to face with a girl about her age, who did a visible double take before her face resumed a pleasant half smile.

The girl possessed the kind of dark Italian beauty that turns heads. She had long waving black hair, tanned skin, liquid brown eyes and carmine lips. She was also effortlessly glamorous in a floaty baby-doll tunic, skinny jeans and a pair of camel wedge sandals with impossibly high heels.

Janey was so tired that it took her a long moment to register that the girl was *not* Celia Albright. 'I'm sorry, you are . . . ?' She hesitated.

'I could ask you the same question!' the girl replied, smiling. 'But I wouldn't have to.' She gestured for Janey to follow her through the ornate doorway of 2C. 'I've been expecting you for *hours*, darling. You're lucky to even make it inside, because I was about to give up and head out for lunch with my friends and *you've* got no key. I was afraid it was going to be ships passing in the night.'

She gave a little laugh, breezing ahead of Janey without bothering to introduce herself or to give a tour of the glorious, high-ceilinged apartment they were walking through, as though Janey had seen it all before. Janey had to remind herself to close her mouth. *This was home for the next two weeks?*

'This is your room,' the girl indicated. 'Bathroom's over there.'

She sailed out again and left Janey to look around the bedroom, which contained a beautiful antique bed piled high with pillows and ivory linen, a lovely old bedside table with a pile of classic Australian novels on it, and a battered leather armchair. The room was probably one of the apartment's smaller ones, with a view over a busy street corner into several other graceful old apartment buildings, rather than the internal courtyard garden in which fountains played. But Janey loved every bit of it.

While she was unpacking her clothes into the built-in wardrobe with sliding mirrored doors that took up one whole wall, she heard the buzzer sound several times, followed by different voices breaking into Italian.

Heading out to the bathroom to put down her toiletry bag, Janey was waylaid by the girl and four of her friends, two other girls and two boys.

'This is her,' the girl smiled. Pointing a finger at each of the teenagers, she said for Janey's benefit, 'Paolo, Brandon, Minka and Luz.' Janey nodded as she found herself at the receiving end of several interested stares.

'Hello Jane,' said one of the boys finally, in an American accent. 'I'm Brandon.'

A little flustered, Janey registered that he was very, *very* cute, in a preppy, blond, tanned, all-American kind of way, and that she was still clutching her toiletry bag in front of her, like an idiot.

'Everyone calls me Janey,' she replied shyly, shifting it into her left hand and holding out her right.

'That's not the way we do things here, Janey,' said Brandon. Without warning, he grabbed Janey close and gave her a kiss, first on one cheek, then the other, while the dark-haired girl and her other friends looked on in amusement. Janey blushed in confusion as Brandon let her go and stepped back.

'The poor darling's been flying for *hours*,' the girl exclaimed to her friends as they prepared to leave the apartment. 'Now get some shut-eye, Janey. Catch you later!'

Then the apartment door closed with a click and Janey's sluggish brain ground into gear with the realisation that the girl must be Freddy, Celia's daughter — although she looked nothing like her — and that the gorgeously dressed teens had to be friends from the posh international school Freddy attended. For a moment, she envied their witty ease with the Italian language, wondering what they'd been bantering about among themselves when they'd arrived.

Wearily, Janey poked her head into each of the spacious rooms in order to get a feel for the layout of the apartment, noting the beautiful antiques mixed in with cutting-edge Danish modern furniture and quirky ornaments gathered from far-flung places.

Feeling a bit fuzzy, she returned to her bedroom and lay down, intending to take a short nap. She wanted to be a little more clear-headed for Celia's arrival.

But when Celia arrived home hours later, Janey was still out like a light.

Via Veneto

For a good ten seconds after Janey woke the next morning, she wasn't sure where she was or what she could possibly be doing there. The art deco ceiling of the elegant room was beautiful but totally unfamiliar, and warm summer sunshine streamed in from the tall windows beside her queen-sized bed.

As she registered that she'd not only fallen asleep in the clothes she was wearing the day before (and the day before that!), but had also drooled in her sleep, Janey sat bolt upright with a groan.

'Talk about making a great first impression!' she said aloud. 'Janey Gordon, once again, is all *class*.'

Getting shakily to her feet, she headed out to the kitchen. The quality of the silence in the apartment told her that she was on her own. Freddy had evidently gone out again with her posse of beautiful besties, and Aunt Celia, it turned out, had left Janey a note and a pair of keys. The note was propped up against a coffee machine that had been loaded to the brim. Janey helped herself to a mug of strong black coffee, and sat down at the high marble kitchen bench to read the note in Celia's strong hand.

> *Janey dear,*
> *So sorry to have missed you,*
> *but didn't want to wake you.*
> *You looked all done in.*

'And,' Janey muttered into her coffee, 'you seemed to be drooling in your sleep, so I left you to it!' She shook her head with a rueful grin and continued scanning the note.

> *Can't make breakfast with you today,*
> *I'm afraid - meetings, meetings, meetings - but we'll have dinner tonight at my favourite trattoria, shall we? Food's fantastic, it isn't dressy,*
>   *and we'll have all the time in the world to catch up.*
>   *Luca will swing by for you at 8.*
> *We eat late here, as I'm sure you know.*

Janey's mouth curved into a big smile at the mention of Luca. The restaurant might not be worth dressing up for, but it didn't mean she wouldn't make an effort!

Big key's for the security door, small key's for the apartment.
Suggest you take a bus down the Via Nomentana. Check it's going in the direction of the centro storico and you'll be right - that's the historical centre, in case your Italian's rusty. Excuse Freddy's absence today, but her school holidays started last week and she had a few things already planned.
I'm sure you two will catch up over the weekend.
Ciao! Ciao!
Celia.

Janey smiled before chug-a-lugging the rest of her coffee and shuffling off to finish unpacking.

After a heavenly shower in the gleaming marble and chrome guest bathroom, Janey dried her hair and tied it back loosely before slipping into the white short shorts, the silky peasant blouse and a pair of comfy leather flip-flops. She accessorised with a couple of chunky red perspex bangles, a pair of silver pirate-style hoop earrings, and a perky black sailor's cap in the manner of boho, foho 'It' girls everywhere. Looking a lot more sophisticated and altogether more Ness-like than she was used to, Janey left the apartment, carrying a black daypack containing an Italian phrase book, a guidebook, her camera, the keys, Ness's spare pair of rockstar sunglasses, and some of the Italian money she'd changed at the airport before boarding the plane.

Janey had the worst singing voice in the world, but she felt like breaking into song as she walked down the villa's grand front steps and looked about at the bustling street scene before her. Thanks to her mega sleep-in, it was almost high noon and cars jostled for space with scooters, which in turn fought for breathing room with pedestrians, trucks, motorbikes and pigeons. The street was crowded on both sides with huge trees and brooding villas with mysterious walled gardens, punctuated by the occasional hole-in-the-wall coffee vendor or dark green, old-style newspaper stand. She'd never seen anything like it. It seemed suddenly as though life had been magnified, like she'd stepped onto the set of a foreign movie.

'Perfect,' said Janey aloud with satisfaction. 'It's just *perfect*.' She slipped the sunglasses on and pulled out her guidebook.

The first order of business had to be brunch. Her growling stomach reminded her that she'd missed at least a couple of meals thanks to her extended snorefest. Flicking through her guidebook, she found that there was some kind of undercover fresh food market not too far away, in the Piazza Alessandria. Because the weather was so beautiful, and there was so much to just drink in, Janey decided to skip the bus ride described in her guidebook and walk there.

At the market, she used a combination of really bad phrasebook Italian and smiling sign language to buy fresh bread, salame, soft cheese, olives and red grapes, blushing a little as the boys manning the stalls tried to flirt with her in broken English. She kept walking as she scoffed her way through her purchases, soon passing through the ancient Porta Salaria, or 'Gate of Salt' – a breach in the towering walls surrounding the historical heart of Rome. The city walls bore the evidence of layers of history all jumbled together. Janey stopped for a moment by the ruins of a tomb that commemorated the life of some eleven-year-old poet prodigy from the first century AD, a time so long ago that she couldn't quite wrap her mind around it. And just like that, she'd entered the old city, flanked by a seething mass of kamikaze traffic.

It felt incredible to have absolutely no agenda for the day, Janey mused, crumpling up her last paper bag before stowing it away in her pack. She couldn't remember a day recently when she'd been so free of responsibility. A sudden surge of sorrow that her mum wasn't here to see the ancient and the new collide so spectacularly made tears spring into her eyes. *She would have loved all this*, thought Janey wistfully. *The mad market, the crazy traffic, all of it.* She blinked furiously before fumbling for her camera, taking a photo of the glorious chaos around her, and walking on down sun-drenched streets in the direction of the famed Via Veneto, which Em had urged her to visit.

'Even if you never see that Fellini movie,' Em had said, 'and it's probably number 581 on your list of things to do before you leave for Rome, at least you can park your bum and have a coffee where most of the people in the film used to hang out in real life. It's a *must-do* street, and not just for sad movie-buffs like me. I have six vital words for you: tiramisù at the Café de Paris. Eat some for me, I beg you.'

Passing one luxury hotel after another on the famous

thoroughfare, Janey was suddenly struck with a fantastic idea. She would call Em and the others, *right now*. She checked her watch and worked out that it was around nine-thirty in the evening back in Australia. At least one of them had to be home.

Janey ducked into The Hotel Majestic, smiling shyly at the liveried doorman who held the door open for her. She was met by a rush of cool, lightly perfumed air. The place was *stuffed* with antiques, towering floral arrangements, and rich-looking old dudes with blingy wives and truckloads of matching luggage. From what she could see, the hotel lived up to its name with bells on.

'Uh, telefono?' she asked the bored-looking concierge, who haughtily lifted an index finger in the direction of the hotel's business centre, a compact space containing a couple of telephone booths and some office equipment, presided over by a serene young woman in a black suit.

The woman explained the rates to Janey in perfect English before motioning her into one of the booths and closing the glass door with a smile.

With excited anticipation, Janey took off her sunglasses and rang Em's number, holding her breath as the call connected. Speaking to her friends was worth the small fortune she would probably have to pay.

'Emily speaking,' said Em in her proper answering-the-phone voice.

'It's your Rome correspondent here,' said Janey breathlessly, 'reporting to you live and direct from . . . Fellini central!'

Janey felt sure Em's answering shriek could be heard with arctic disapproval in the hushed reception area. As it was, the young woman sitting just outside the phone booth raised her head briefly and smiled before returning her gaze to the fax she was reading.

'*OMG!*' Em squealed, back once more in over-the-top Em-mode. 'I was just thinking of you, Janes! You're the spookiest mind-reader *ever*! What time is it there? Where have you been? What have you seen? What have you eaten? How's the mysterious aunt? What's her pad like? Mega plush? Plush? Or just semi-plush?'

'Slow down! Slow down!' Janey laughed, thinking with a pang how good it was to hear her friend's voice. 'I'm – at this very moment – sitting in a nicely appointed phone booth in a five-star hotel in the epicentre of *your* must-do street, if you must know. Haven't tried the coffee around here yet, but I think that and a big fat serve of tiramisù are definitely next on my list. It's about one-thirty in the arvo, my yummy paper bag brunch is a very distant memory, I've already eyeballed more Roman ruins than you could shake a stick at, and I *still* haven't actually sighted or spoken with my mysterious aunt. Fell asleep soon as I got here,' Janey added sheepishly. 'Missed her again this morning. And her pad is *off* the mega-plush end of the spectrum. Her building's even got one of those lifts you see in 1950s spy movies!'

Em sighed. 'I want photographic proof of *everything*, Jane Gordon. I'm giving you permission to bore me to death with your holiday snaps as soon as you get back because it can't be any worse than what I'm going through right now! Gabs is away at her grandmother's beach house this weekend, and Ness is – you guessed it – working her night shift at the cinema to save up for the latest Chloé "It" bag, so I'm drowning my sorrows in microwave popcorn and '90s slacker movies. How sad is that? I was, like, *two* when some of these were made. So seriously, are you totally loving it?'

'Apart from Ness's walk-in wardrobe, it has to be the most amazing place I've ever seen! You can't go three steps without falling over a Roman ruin, or a crazed Vespa driver. I never thought I'd be so completely in love with a place! Not to mention meeting the guy of my dreams ten seconds after leaving the airport . . .' Janey added tantalisingly.

'You can't be serious?' Em interrupted.

'Get this! I walk out the airport doors and he's standing there holding a sign with my name on it and murmuring, "I'd know you *anywhere*, signorina." And not only that, Em, he's *total* crush material from head to toe! Tall, dark, gorgeous, and dressed like an international man of mystery. The real kind,' Janey laughed, 'not the Austin Powers kind.'

'Who *is* he?' Em breathed. 'He knew who you were?'

'He's my aunt's personal chauffeur, Luca,' said Janey. 'Even his *name's* divine! *And* he's picking me up tonight at eight . . . but only to take me to my aunt of course.

'He probably doesn't even remember what I look like, Em,' she added. 'He's the sort who deals with sophisticated people all day, all year round. If you've ever seen an elegant Roman woman in full war paint, big hair and designer gear – and I passed plenty on my way here – someone who looks like me wouldn't even rate a second glance! As soon as he dropped me at my aunt's place, I'm sure he pretty much forgot I existed.'

'You'd be surprised, Janey,' Em replied. 'Since Ness performed emergency wardrobe surgery on you that night, and you started trial-running the principles of high fashion during the last week of school, even Cameron Mallory and his too-cool-for-school skater crew were suddenly asking about you.'

'Are you kidding?' Janey shot back with disbelief. Cameron Mallory and his skater boy buddies were the hottest Year 12 guys at Selbourne High. They never noticed *anybody*, mainly because they didn't have to. Every guy wanted to hang out with them. Every girl, from the smallest Year 7 pipsqueak upwards, wanted to date them.

'Believe it,' said Em. 'Apparently, a millisecond after you walked by him on the last day of school in that very Jessica Simpson-esque ensemble you were wearing, he was asking Jenny Kyriacou's older brother who on earth you were. Like you haven't been part of the school furniture since, well, *forever*! It was pure genius to throw your long cardie over that grey T-shirt dress Ness lent you. And only someone with stick legs like yours could get away with wearing black tights and red open-toed wedges. In *winter*.'

Janey snorted. 'He was probably asking, Emily, because I trod on his toes as I clomped past. I almost did a Naomi Campbell off those platforms that afternoon, that's how out of control I was in them! If Gabs hadn't grabbed me by the elbow

I would've fallen flat on my face as the final bell went.'

'Well, believe what you like, Janes, but if you keep up this whole dressing-like-a-Hollywood-starlet thing, don't be surprised if Cam Mallory suddenly sails up to you on his Dogtown skateboard next term and asks for your phone number,' said Em loyally. 'Jenny said he sounded pretty keen to get to know you. And we *do* have an end-of-year formal coming up. You could do worse. *Way* worse.'

'Don't do my head in!' Janey turned as the hotel employee tapped on the glass door of the phone booth and indicated that she was about to be charged for a second block of time. 'Gotta go,' Janey said, miming her thanks at the young woman. 'Apparently I'm about to blow a second huge chunk of change if I don't get off now. And I *really* want that tiramisù that I promised to eat for you! Tell the others I'll try to call again.'

'Soon as you get back to luxury central, check out if your aunt has a computer,' Em advised. 'She should, if your description of her pad is anything to go by. If my calculations are correct, I'll tell the others to expect a bit of MySpace or telephone action from you either really early or really late our time.'

'You got it,' Janey replied. She replaced the heavy black old-style receiver in its cradle. It suddenly struck her how far away her besties were. Rome would be ten thousand times more breathtaking than it was already if those guys were here as well. She was so used to sharing everything with them, highs *and* lows. She felt her eyes misting again, and had to compose herself before leaving the booth.

Janey grabbed her sunnies, paid her phone tab with a smile, and walked quickly back across the reception area towards the revolving front door of the hotel. But before she could enter it, she heard someone call out her name. Janey spun around in surprise.

'Thought it was you,' drawled the tall, blond young man in a confident American accent, looking Janey up and down appreciatively. He took off his Ray-Bans and slicked back his perfect hair with one tanned hand. 'Brandon, remember?'

Janey coloured. Freddy's friend, the preppy guy with the amazing sky-blue eyes. Of course, he had to stand there looking like a male model, while, thanks to her long walk and her conversation with Em, she looked like a sweaty, shiny, emotional fur ball. Janey wondered why he'd even bothered to call out to her.

'Mmm-hmmm,' she said. 'Um, fancy meeting *you* here.' She winced at how lame she sounded, just wanting to escape.

Brandon surprised her by apologising. 'Look, I'm sorry if I made you feel uncomfortable yesterday, grabbing you like that. I forget how full-on we can all be! Especially Freddy, who can be a pretty forceful character. You're both so ... *different*. It's hard to believe you're related.'

Janey blushed even more wildly.

'I meant that in a *good* way,' he said hastily. 'Look, can I buy you a coffee? I can feel foot-in-mouth happening again. You have this effect on me ...'

Janey shot him a look of pure astonishment and Brandon

laughed. 'Honestly, there's something about you, Jane, that makes me say and do all the wrong stuff. Let's start over?'

'Uh, my friends call me Janey, and I've already got a date, s-sorry, and I'm pretty keen to keep it.'

But Brandon wouldn't be deterred. 'Would he mind if I crashed it?'

The determination on his face made Janey burst out in giggles, despite how uncomfortable she was feeling. 'It isn't with a *he*, but with a giant serving of tiramisù. At the Café de Paris. I promised someone I'd make haste there forthwith and genteelly stuff my face with it. You can come along if you want. But it won't be pretty!'

Brandon's shoulders relaxed, and he gave a pearly-white grin. 'I'd like that. I haven't been there in ages and I can't imagine anyone better to share a very rich, very fattening dessert with.'

For a moment, Freddy's flawless features bobbed up in Janey's mind and her smile died. There was someone better, right there. She sighed inwardly before tucking escaped tendrils of hair back under her cap and saying brightly, 'Lead the way!'

Janey and Brandon spent so long laughing over coffee and cake at the Café de Paris that she had to sprint like a madwoman to make it back to Celia's apartment in time to have a shower before meeting her aunt for dinner. The day had already brought a surprise new acquaintance, not to mention an avalanche of new sights, tastes and experiences, and Janey couldn't believe there was still more to come!

She began to feel really nervous about finally meeting her aunt, and it took her ages to work out what to wear. She finally settled on the classic red-and-white striped halter-neck top and skinny jeans, cramming her feet into the red wedges and praying silently that she wouldn't topple out of them right under Luca's nose. After achieving the usual slightly lopsided results with her hair straightener, she tied a jaunty silk scarf around her neck and let herself out of the apartment just before eight. She walked carefully down the front steps of the villa at the same time that Luca pulled up at the kerb in the shiny black car.

Luca slid elegantly out of the driver's seat and held Janey's door open for her as though she were visiting royalty. 'Ciao bella!' he said, as Janey slid into the front passenger seat, glad she hadn't lost control of her treacherous footwear.

He didn't really mean the 'bella' bit, she told herself sternly. *He's just being polite.* But her heart felt like it had skipped a beat regardless.

Luca turned the car in the direction of Celia Albright's favourite trattoria, Da Edoardo. But he had to charm Janey into telling him about her day, because all of a sudden she was tongue-tied. She'd been looking forward to seeing Luca all day, and now here he was, and here she was, and the trip was probably half over already, and she'd probably never see him again after today and, well, what was the point anyway?

As the car entered Rome's old city once more, and Janey couldn't manage anything more than one-word answers, Luca began talking about himself, and how he was taking time off from his second year of architectural studies at the University of Rome to indulge his passion for meeting people from around the world, and to figure out what he really wanted to do.

'I am lazy, no?' he laughed. 'At least, my father, he think so. He is quite the famous *architetto* here, in this country, and he is angry that I "waste my life". But I enjoy very much the driving, and to talk with new people.'

'Will you go back, do you think?' Janey asked, her interest piqued. 'I'm hoping to do, um, journalism or psychology one day. My friends seem to think I'm a good listener . . .'

'Perhaps, in time,' Luca replied airily, avoiding a bus that swung out without warning from the kerb. 'But not yet, I think. The Australians, they are good to me. I meet many interesting people from your country, some I have even visit, in Sydney, Perth, your Great Reef.'

'The Great *Barrier* Reef?' Janey exclaimed as Luca nodded. 'I haven't even been there yet!'

And despite herself, Janey started to describe her day – fluffing her Italian verbs at the undercover market, her long walk, braving the super luxe Hotel Majestic. 'And would you believe I met one of Freddy's friends there when I went in to use the phone?' she said. 'He just happened to be there – visiting his uncle – isn't that incredible?'

Luca glanced sidelong at Janey as he negotiated another impossible overtake. '*Veramente*? It is indeed incredible, signorina. Rome is a big city. Chi? Who was it?'

'Brandon,' said Janey happily. 'The male modelly one, not the horrible one – Paolo, I think his name was – who looked at me like I was something stuck to the bottom of his shoe. Brandon and I had afternoon tea at the Café de Paris. He even gave me his mobile number! I thought he'd be a bit stuck up, looking the way he looks, but he's not. He's actually really, really nice.'

Janey still couldn't believe how much she and Brandon had had in common and how the afternoon had flown by. He rocked out to the same bands she was into (The Killers, Franz Ferdinand, Good Charlotte, Powderfinger), loved reading trashy thrillers like she did, and had lost his mum at a really young age as well. The similarities between their lives – apart from the fact that Brandon's dad was a mega-wealthy industrialist from the east coast of America who was currently based in Italy doing million-dollar business deals – were *amazing*.

'Why are you surprised that this Brandon, he is nice? You are not "stuck up", as you say, yet you are also——?' Luca hadn't finished his sentence before Janey burst out laughing.

'It's lovely of you to even suggest that I'm remotely as good-looking as Brandon is. But it's just the clothes, Luca. Until this week, I was a fashion dyslexic!'

Luca shot her a puzzled look as he prepared to make a right turn past a cluster of haphazardly parked Vespas into a narrow one-way street. 'I do not understand you?' he said.

'No, you wouldn't,' Janey continued, amazed at how her

life was suddenly filled with cute guys who seemed totally interested in *her*. The Janey of last week seemed a whole lifetime away.

Note to self, she thought. *Do something nice for Ness when you get home. She so deserves it.*

The thought of having to return home soon made Janey's smile dim a little, and it disappeared altogether when Luca announced, 'We're here, signorina.'

Celia

Luca swung his lean, athletic frame out of the car and opened Janey's door, pointing out the brightly lit trattoria where her aunt would be waiting. He shot Janey his usual dazzling smile before jumping back into the car and roaring off up a narrow side street that was little more than a cobbled laneway.

'Well, that's it then,' Janey told herself a bit forlornly as Luca's tail-lights vanished. 'That's probably the last time you'll ever see him, so stop being stupid, *stupid*.'

She turned her attention back to the tiny piazza where Da Edoardo was located and her mood began to lift. It was one of a string of buzzing eateries facing onto the miniature square and its sparkling, central fountain. Sidewalk tables spilled out in all directions, crowded with local families and couples of every description enjoying a Friday night out.

She navigated her way past the trattoria's crowded entrance and scanned the bustling restaurant for her aunt.

'Buonasera, signorina!' winked a passing waiter, who was loaded up with plates of glorious looking pasta. 'Sua madre è lì.' He made a vague gesture towards the rear of the trattoria and kept moving.

'I'm sorry?' Janey shouted after him. The only Italian she knew off by heart pretty much consisted of food words and definitely *no* verbs or anything vaguely resembling a whole sentence.

'She is there,' shouted the barman as he deftly poured jewel-coloured apéritifs. 'You mother.' Again, the man gestured towards the rear of the restaurant.

'My mother?' said Janey blankly, thinking for one heart-stopping moment that she would look across the room and Lydia would be sitting there.

She blinked away the sudden tears in her eyes, finally spotting the woman from the photo waving at her excitedly from the back of the room.

Janey waved back, her astonishment growing the closer she came to her aunt's table. It was extraordinary how alike they looked.

'You must be Janey!' said Celia warmly, similar astonishment gripping her very familiar features. She stood up and gave Janey a bear hug that nearly lifted her off her feet.

Janey hugged her aunt back, noting that they were almost the same height and that underneath all the polish, her aunt really *did* possess the same fly-away hair and freckles that she did.

It was deeply freaky how alike they looked, although Celia's eyes were brown while Janey's were a clear grey-blue. She decided that her aunt looked kind, capable and rather friendly, and some of her tension ebbed. Even if Celia was practically a stranger, it felt so good to have *some* family again. Even an unconventional kind. At that moment, she felt happier than she had been in a long while, smiling as Celia poured her a glass of water and fussed over her exactly as Lydia would have done.

They sat and stared at each other for a while. Celia was beautifully dressed in a russet-coloured sleeveless shift and discreet gold jewellery. The latest Fendi handbag in black patent leather was slung casually over the back of her chair, and a pile of papers spilled out untidily from the document wallet that lay on the table.

'Boring stuff that shouldn't be here,' Celia smiled, tidying the papers away into the wallet and turning her warm gaze back on her niece.

'I can see how the waiters made the mistake of thinking that you and I are, um . . .' Janey hesitated.

'It's uncanny,' Celia agreed. 'They've all seen Freddy and I here, dozens of times, but as soon as they clapped eyes on you they just assumed I'd been hiding a secret love child somewhere!'

'My mum did that job for you!' Janey smiled, a little sadly.

'She certainly did,' Celia replied. 'And so well that we mightn't have met at all if you hadn't found my lawyer's letter! I'm so glad you're here. You don't know *how* glad. I've often wondered about Lydia, where she was, what she was doing, what she was like. And now here *we* are.'

Celia looked a little misty herself before recovering and signalling for a waiter. 'This is a celebration!' she said. 'So we shall act accordingly. I've just told Marco to bring on the artichokes.'

At Janey's perplexed expression, Celia chuckled and said, 'They *are* a food and, trust me, you *will* like them.'

As the evening wore on, both Janey and Celia stuffed themselves silly with a host of amazing things – salt cod fritters, veal with anchovy sauce, fried zucchini flowers and rabbit stewed with apricots – that Janey had never in her life tried before, and in some cases had never even heard of.

'Gabs – one of my best friends in the world, who is a foodie *tragic* – won't believe the things I've eaten tonight,' said Janey. She groaned as another large platter of Roman delicacies was plonked on the table in front of her, before taking a tentative bite. 'Who knew that – I can't believe I'm saying this – *tripe* could be so, uh, delicious?'

'You can call and tell her all about it after we get home,' Celia offered. 'Or email her. There's a computer in the study. My login isn't passworded because I usually use my embassy laptop if I need to contact someone. We've also got Skype, if you know what that is and how to use it.'

Janey's answering grin said it all. Email was so *yesterday*. 'If it's okay with you, uh, Aunt Celia,' she replied, still getting used to the word 'aunt', 'I'll definitely use it. Sometimes, actual face time *is* the only way.'

'Be my guest. I hardly use it anyway. I spend half the day video conferencing at work so only Freddy gives the home headset and webcam a real workout. You'll have to fight her for airtime though,' Celia warned. 'She's a MySpace junkie.'

As she spoke, she slid a huge portion of rich goose tart onto Janey's plate. Janey tried not to look horrified as she picked up her fork.

'I just wanted you to try some real, seasonal, local food,' Celia laughed, noting Janey's expression. 'Not the greasy, cheesy fare they serve up in the tourist traps that masquerades as Roman cuisine. Now eat up! This is a real treat for the tastebuds.'

Janey took a deep breath and dug in.

'I'm sorry Freddy isn't here,' said Celia, 'but she's staying the night at her father's. My ex-husband, Angelo, lives about fifteen minutes from my place. It's part of the reason I'm now based in Rome – I wanted Freddy to spend more time with her father. He was an Italian diplomat based overseas, but now works with the interior ministry. She doesn't seem to want to spend much time with me at the moment,' Celia added a bit stiffly, 'because she blames *me* for the split, even though splits are usually, by definition, *two* sides deciding to go their separate ways.'

Janey listened with interest. It would explain why Freddy looked nothing like her mum at all and resembled a junior Milanese catwalk model. She'd obviously inherited her father's exotic looks and colouring.

'We broke up,' Celia continued grimly, 'because Angelo's expectations changed. He suddenly decided that he wanted the traditional full-time, stay-at-home wife and mother, neatly forgetting that the whole reason we'd met in the first place was because I'd been seconded to the United Nations in New York, just like he had! I've actually had to give up a more senior posting in Paris to give Freddy more time with both of us. It's the kind of dilemma men don't usually have to face, frankly.'

'But enough heavy stuff!' Celia added, as Janey tried to disguise her still loaded plate with her napkin. 'I'm just glad you're here. It's *so* important to me that you and Freddy get to know each other and that you get along.' She gave Janey a searching look. 'And you'll be great company for Freddy during the holidays. I'm working to all sorts of impossible deadlines at the moment.'

Janey doubted Freddy needed her company at all, but it was lovely of Celia to say so.

Celia looked as though she wanted to say something important, but instead signalled to Marco to bring coffee and dessert. 'My mum – my adoptive mother – first got me hooked on real Italian coffee, even though we were living on a military base in the Philippines in those days and luxuries were hard to come by.'

Janey listened wide-eyed as Celia detailed her childhood with her adoptive parents, who'd never been able to have kids naturally.

'Dad was in the air force,' Celia explained, 'so we moved

around a lot. I went to six different high schools in almost as many countries, which was *the* best preparation for life in the diplomatic corps! I really caught the travel bug early and I haven't managed to shake it yet.'

'Apart from Mum's vanishing act with me,' said Janey, eyeing the dessert tray that had appeared before them with slight dread, 'we never went anywhere . . . not that I'm complaining. It's just the way things were. I've known Gabs almost my whole life. And my other two best friends – Emily and Ness – I met on my first day in high school. I can't imagine not having them in my life, if you see what I mean. I wish you could meet them.'

'You're lucky to have friendships like that,' said Celia. 'I often wonder whether Freddy would be less angry with me, and with life in general, if I hadn't moved her around the world so much.'

'She's fifteen, right?' said Janey. 'Everyone's angry all the time when they're fifteen. It's just life, she'll get over it.'

'She's almost sixteen.' Celia smiled, a touch sadly. 'And we've been fighting like cats and dogs lately. I hope you're right. Now eat up that zabaione! It's a house special.'

Janey picked up her spoon. 'What were they like? My, um, grandparents,' she said, feeling like a traitor for asking. The word felt very strange in her mouth.

From zero family to having a secret history, almost overnight, Janey thought to herself. It was *crazy*.

'Mum never talked about them much,' she added. 'They hurt her pretty badly, I think, at a time when she needed them most.'

A funny look flitted across Celia's face again, but the look vanished and she shrugged. 'Bitter, disappointed, still angry at Lydia after all that time. Angry that she left, angry that she stayed away. At first I didn't want to meet them because I didn't want to get involved. The whole story was too sad. But my adoptive mother – my real mum in every way that matters – gave me her blessing and said my parents, your grandparents, should be given the opportunity to say what they wanted to say, that everyone deserves the chance to clear their conscience. But it wasn't their consciences that troubled them! What kept them awake at night was the fact they no longer had a blood heir to leave their fortune to. I was the only candidate left. Not the most desirable one, admittedly – I was practically a stranger, with a "lower-class" upbringing – but there you go. I was still "blood".'

Janey had trouble swallowing for moment, even though the chocolate amaretti cake she was sampling was as light as air. 'That fortune could've kept my mother alive for a little bit longer,' she muttered in quiet distress. 'There was so much she still wanted to do, but time just ran out.' She hung her head.

Celia reached over and grasped Janey's hands. 'Your grandparents' will was the most complex piece of work you could ever imagine,' she murmured. 'It was a headache I could've done without! And it came with a stately, triple-storey waterfront townhouse in Sydney, a massive country estate in the Hunter Valley, together with a vast collection of artworks, a vintage car collection and a huge cellar of wine amassed from around the globe! What's a lowly government pen-pusher like me supposed to do with a crazy fortune like that?' Celia gave a strained laugh, a strange look passing across her features once again.

Janey's eyes welled at the thought of her valiant teenage mum giving up a life of enormous privilege just to have and keep her, and she suddenly missed her more than ever. Though she told herself fiercely to get it together, to her horror, a big, fat tear rolled down her cheek and splashed onto the red-and-white tablecloth in front of her. Celia *had* to have noticed, she thought in mortification as she grabbed at her napkin and pretended to scrub an imaginary bit of food off her face.

Celia wasn't fooled, shooting her niece a quick, sidelong look that took in everything from Janey's damp eyelashes to her flushed cheeks. But she acted as though she hadn't seen a thing, ordering kindly, 'Now stop pretending to eat your dessert and take this.'

Janey managed a soggy grin, put down her napkin and took the mobile phone that Celia was proffering over the table.

'It's an Italian cell phone,' Celia explained. 'Pre-programmed with the telephone numbers of my office at the embassy, my cell phone, Freddy's cell phone and, for emergencies, Luca's cell phone number.'

Janey's face lit up at the mention of Luca, and Celia frowned. 'Only call the last number if you're seriously stranded and need help,' she insisted. 'Luca's primarily the Ambassador's driver, so he's absolutely off limits during business hours if your "emergency" is too many shopping bags or a broken stiletto.'

'Of course,' Janey agreed, though she had to concentrate hard to stop herself breaking out into a wide smile. She had his number! And she hadn't even had to get up the courage to ask him for it.

As Janey took a last sip of her coffee, her mind on Luca and where he could possibly be right now, Celia picked up her own mobile phone and spoke briefly into it in rapid-fire Italian.

'I was going to arrange for Luca to come back and pick us up tonight,' she said after she hung up, 'but it's such a beautiful evening that I think we'll walk instead. The apartment isn't far. Maybe twenty minutes from here. I've just told Luca to clock off for the day.'

For a moment, Janey couldn't hide her disappointment and Celia frowned again.

'Don't get too close to Luca Sarti, Jane Gordon,' she warned gently, 'because he's a twenty-one-year-old smoothie who's *way* out of your league, with a BlackBerry full of dates with European glamazons to prove it. I'd trust him with my life and yours, don't get me wrong. He's a sweetie, and an absolute gentleman. But he can't be trusted not to *break your heart*. Just ask Freddy if you don't believe me. She's been tying herself in knots trying to get his attention for months, and so far it hasn't worked.'

A suddenly awkward silence fell over the table as Celia and Janey gathered up their things to leave.

Circus Maximus

When Janey rolled out of bed late on Saturday morning in her tatty Mr Happy shortie PJs, she was astonished to find Freddy in the kitchen, wearing a blinged-up Victoria's Secret pink hoodie and matching sweatpants, preparing a mouth-watering hot brunch.

Freddy looked her up and down, but not in an unfriendly way. 'Sorry I haven't been around. Mum's out – *as usual* – so I thought I'd make us something to eat.'

Janey looked down at the plate that Freddy was sliding across the table at her. 'Poached eggs, smoked salmon, spinach and rosti,' Freddy smiled. 'A girl's gotta eat! Knives and forks are over there. Help yourself to coffee.'

She's just trying to be friends, Janey told herself as she found some cutlery and a mug, even though part of her was unsure why. Janey's first impressions of people were usually spot on, and her first impression of Freddy hadn't screamed *potential bestie*. More like: *here's a super style queen who probably wouldn't be caught dead being seen with me, even in a parallel universe.*

The two girls dug into their meals, silently eyeing each other over the marble benchtop with curiosity.

'You know, your hair's such a great colour. You could do so much more with it,' Freddy commented finally. Her own hair of course, was rippling in perfectly styled waves down her back even though she'd just gotten out of bed.

Janey wrinkled her nose. 'Tell that to my straightener.'

'You've got to show it who's boss,' Freddy laughed. 'You should've seen me when I got my first one! A good dose of anti-frizz serum and styling solution helps as well. I'll show you after we eat.'

After the two girls finished up in the kitchen, with Freddy doing the washing and Janey drying, Freddy was as good as her word. She took Janey down the hall to her over-the-top double bedroom, which looked like something out of a Versace homewares catalogue, and ordered Janey to sit down at the huge 1930s dressing table covered in designer-label cosmetics and shopping bags.

'Clean hair is a must,' said Freddy knowledgeably, 'and it goes without saying that you need *the best* thermal protection spray and anti-frizz serum you can find, like these ones.' Freddy smeared solution out of some brightly coloured bottles all over Janey's hair and then sectioned it into workable chunks, using ibis clips to keep each bit separate. 'And a *ghd* styler is the only way to go, in my opinion,' Freddy added. 'Anything else just *won't* give you the same results.'

Janey listened politely as Freddy twisted her hair into neat sections. As Freddy was doing her best to be friendly, Janey didn't bother telling her that a *ghd* styler was something her pocket money had never stretched to, let alone the name brand serums Freddy was lavishly working into her hair from root to tip.

'For sleek and straight, really concentrate on the front sections,' Freddy continued, pulling her styling iron through one section of Janey's hair at a time. 'It's all about initial impact. For BIG hair you need to work in volumiser and hairspray as well *before* you start styling each section *away* from your scalp. Finish with shine serum and there you have it.' Freddy's eyes met Janey's in the mirror. 'International hair like mine.'

She stared at Janey's reflection. 'Well, not exactly like mine. You're right, your hair really *is* impossible.'

'It won't do what it's told,' Janey responded, smiling. 'But it looks heaps better than it does usually. Thanks.' She gave her hair a little shake and watched as it rippled about her shoulders. It would probably frizz up in about five seconds, but for a moment, she looked kind of *hot*.

'It's as bad as Mum's hair,' Freddy grinned in agreement. 'I'm *so* happy I missed out on that unfortunate bit of the Gordon gene pool.'

Janey stiffened at the comment, trying not to appear hurt. *Freddy could use a serious crash course at charm school*, she thought, *but she means well.*

She refocused on her glossy new hairdo and found Freddy staring at her again in the mirror. 'There's a rave party tonight at the Circo Massimo,' said Freddy. 'The Circus Maximus to non-Italians. Everyone I know is going to be there and it kicks off at ten. Wanna come? It'll be a *blast*. It's probably not your bag...'

Janey tried not to look startled. 'Uh,' she replied. She'd never been to a dance party. None of her friends were into that scene back home, and even if they'd wanted to, their parents wouldn't have let them anywhere near it! Sleepovers and pool parties were more their thing.

'You know, *a rave*,' Freddy explained patiently, when Janey didn't say *yes* immediately. 'A big dance party with electronica, lights, dry ice, VJs, lasers, techno, happy hardcore, trance, Old Skool beats, drum 'n' bass, house. The Circus Maximus has got to be *the* best rave venue in the world. You can fit thousands of people into this huge space that used to be used by the ancient Romans for chariot racing. So do you want to come? It's the *biggest* trip.'

'Uh, yeah, I guess,' said Janey, blinking, as the idea that she, Janey Gordon, would be going to a *rave* slowly sank in. 'That sounds kind of fantastic.'

'It will be wilder than you could ever imagine!' said Freddy. 'It'll *blow* your little mind. There'll be at least five different arenas. It'll be massive! My girls are meeting us there. Paolo can't make it tonight though, pity...'

Great, thought Janey, who hadn't fancied partying with that creep.

'. . . but Brandon's coming after midnight. He's got another party to go to beforehand.'

Janey blushed a little at the mention of Brandon's name, her heartbeat kicking up a notch. Freddy smiled again. 'Like him, do you? Luz says he's *way* too hot for you, but you never know. *I* think she's just jealous, because I could've sworn I noticed some definite two-way chemistry when he pulled you into that clinch!' She ran a brush through Janey's shining, still perfectly obedient hair, and winked.

Janey grinned, but didn't reply. Obviously, Brandon hadn't bothered to update his social set on his secret, sort-of date with her at the Café de Paris. Or the fact that he'd given Janey his mobile number and she already had it programmed into her phone. Janey hugged the knowledge to herself, hoping the afternoon they'd spent together had been just as special to him as it had been to her.

'Luz is probably right,' Janey agreed, wondering what else Freddy's snobby friend had said about her behind her back. 'He's way, *way* too hot for me. But, yes, I'd love to go to the rave.' Getting up and backing out of Freddy's room, she said, 'I'll just go and see what I have to wear.'

Excitement levels rising, Janey headed back to her bedroom and studied the clothes she had, wondering what would work best for a rave. She almost screamed as she brought the beautiful vintage shift Ness had lent her out of the wardrobe and found Freddy standing just behind her, frowning.

'I didn't even hear you come in!' Janey gasped as Freddy examined the shift and shook her head.

'You can't wear *that* to the rave!' Freddy exclaimed. 'Not if you want to make Brandon sit up and take notice, and Luz eat her words.'

She stepped around her taller cousin and flicked through every piece of clothing hanging in Janey's wardrobe as though she were an A-list Hollywood stylist on a last-minute awards night makeover mission.

'No, no, no, *definitely* no, and *absolutely* no.' Freddy fingered the wrap dress as if it were something that had died and begun to smell. 'It's not a *tea party*, Janey. You're aiming for "drive him wild", not polite indifference.'

'What do you suggest then?' Janey said a touch desperately, as Freddy reached the end of her borrowed wardrobe with a look of concern.

'I'll style you for the rave from my own stuff.' Freddy spun on her heel and fixed Janey with her dark, level gaze. 'Everything you've brought along to wear is *so* wrong for tonight. Let me help! I've got tonnes of clothes – we're sure to find something that'll cause a sensation.'

'Uh, okay,' said Janey hesitantly, as Freddy grabbed her by the hem of her very uncool PJs and dragged her back down the hallway.

It took almost all afternoon for Freddy to be satisfied with both their reflections in the full-length mirrors flanking the entry-way to her spacious walk-in wardrobe.

Of course, Freddy looked catwalk-ready in a navy sequined

mini-shift and towering gladiator sandals that showed off her long, honey-coloured limbs and 'international' hair to perfection.

Janey though, wasn't so sure about how she looked. She *did* like the way that Freddy had done her make-up – giving her dramatic, smoky eyes and a strong lip in a glittery bronze-based palette that really brought out her features. Thanks also to Freddy's earlier efforts, her hair still looked fantastically sleek. And Freddy had fi nally deemed her a knockout! But Janey still wasn't completely sold on her overall silhouette. For one thing, the tiny, red, frayed-hem mini she was wearing just made her freckly white legs look even longer and more pale and freckly than they did already. And her leopard print baby-doll top made her usually flat chest look *enormous*. Her whole upper half seemed so, well, *spotty*.

'You don't think this whole thing makes me look, erm, *round?*' She twisted around and saw that her back view was just as lollipop-like as her front.

'You? Little Miss Pencil Legs?' Freddy shrieked in disbelief. They grinned at each other.

'I've given you some *volume*,' said Freddy. 'You totally needed it! *Now* you look great, very jet set Euro princess. *Everyone* is doing animal print at the moment. Now slip these on your feet and we're good to go.' She handed Janey a pair of sky-scraping peep-toe Louboutin heels, with their signature hot red soles. They were at least half a size too tight, but Janey squeezed into them anyway.

'These have to be at least, um, eight inches high!' she

exclaimed. With the heels on, she was well over six feet tall. 'I'm not going to be able to dance very well in these,' she said apologetically, reaching to take them off.

Freddy waved at her to keep them on. 'What's important is the overall *package*,' she said fiercely. 'Play to your strengths – those mile-high legs for starters. You look like a model now – so totally couture. And we're meeting the others at the Goa trance arena, which will mostly involve ambient music that you'll only have to stand and wave your arms to. No shuffling required. You'll be fine. Now let's *go*. Luca's meeting us downstairs, like, *yesterday*.' Freddy sounded pretty impatient to see Luca herself.

Janey tried not to break into a dippy grin at the thought of Luca waiting for them at the bottom of the building. It was the perfect start to her night out. Janey felt excitement building in the pit of her stomach at the thought of hitting a real dance party.

As the girls grabbed their tiny wristlet clutches – big enough only for some money and a lipstick – Celia hurtled through the front door, looking harassed. She did a slight double take at the sight of them but adopted an expression of extreme mildness and murmured, 'Off already, darlings? Have fun! And be home by no later than two, won't you? I know these things can go all night, and that all your friends will be there, Federica, but you know our deal.'

Freddy muttered, 'Yes, Mum, I know our deal.'

'Have you got your phones?' said Celia, looking from one girl to the other.

'Uh...' Janey began as Freddy suddenly clenched one of her hands tightly to shut her up, and said sarcastically, 'Yes, Mother. We've got them. So stop worrying and go back to work, like you *always* do. Even though it's the *weekend*.'

An expression of guilt stole briefly across Celia's face while Janey shot her cousin a bemused look, knowing there hadn't been room in the wristlets for anything like a phone. The tension between Freddy and her mother could have been cut with a knife.

'Right then,' said Celia brightly, 'Make sure you take a taxi home together and stick close to each other all evening. I've got to host tonight's cocktail function at the embassy because the Ambassador's flight has been held up in Munich – there's no way he'll get back in time. So there's a lot I have to prep up on if I don't want to put my foot in it. Have a good time...' Her voice trailed off as Freddy wrenched open the front door and pushed Janey out of the apartment.

'But you *know* we don't have our phones!' Janey hissed as they entered the cage lift and descended. 'Are you sure we won't need them?'

'*She* doesn't need to know that!' Freddy snorted. 'Like she cares! And, *no*, we won't need them. You'll be, like, ten seconds from home. Nothing bad's gonna happen. It's the *last* thing you'll need. Just enjoy the night! One of the others will have a phone anyway.'

Both girls stepped out into the balmy night air, Janey negotiating the villa's front steps in her teetering heels as though her life depended upon her every move, because it did! They were even less manoeuverable than the red wedge heels. If she took a step too quickly, her ankles wobbled. She was practically mincing, though it was probably worth it, she thought, if they made her look like a model.

Luca was leaning against the car, laughing into his mobile. He snapped it shut as he caught sight of Freddy and opened the door for her, doing a visible double take when he realised who was clomping up behind.

'Signorina Gordon?' he exclaimed in surprise, his tone not exactly... *flattering*, Janey realised.

'Oh, for heaven's sake call her Janey like the rest of us do – she's not a duchess or anything – and shut your mouth, Luca,' Freddy retorted as she pushed Janey into the back seat, following her in. 'Doesn't she look sensational? Now drop us at the Piazzale Ugo La Malfa entrance to the Circo Massimo. E rapidamente! We're late. Cinderella here was hard to work with. *Very* hard to work with.' Freddy gave Janey a sidelong grin to show that she was just joking.

Janey stared uncomfortably at the back of Luca's head as he settled himself behind the wheel and turned the key in the ignition. She noted his grim expression as he turned his head briefly to check his blind spot before easing into traffic, wondering at the weird vibe she sensed going on between Luca and Freddy.

As the car headed towards the Via Nomentana, Freddy shot Luca a challenging look in the rearview mirror and said, 'So tell us we look good, tesoro mio.'

'You always appear bella, signorina del Gigli,' Luca replied after the briefest of pauses, 'but you should not have permitted signorina Gordon to leave the villa dressed, in this, this *fashion*. Non sembra appropriato . . .' He lapsed into Italian so that Janey would not understand what he was saying.

'What do you mean, it's not *appropriate*?' Freddy replied laughingly in English.

Janey winced. Is *that* what he thought?

'She does not appear as . . . herself, you understand.' Luca spoke to Freddy over Janey's head as if she were not in the car, wilting inside with each word. 'Non c'era niente di più . . . dignitoso?' he said, meeting Freddy's dark gaze in the mirror.

Freddy snorted. '*Dignitoso?* We're going to a *rave*, Luca, not a night at the opera! Get with it, Granddad. She looks *hot*.'

'Hey, *hey!*' Janey interrupted as both pairs of eyes flicked quickly in her direction and away again. 'I'm in the car, too, you know, and I think I look, uh, *fine*.'

Luca's tone was amused. 'You look disastroso, like the car accident. Too much here, too little there, all falling apart.'

His words pulled Janey up short for a second, Fellini's awful car crash avatar flashing up in her mind's eye, before she shook the image away. When what Luca was saying actually registered, Janey gasped indignantly.

Luca compounded the awfulness by adding a moment later, 'Like you are, how do you say, becoming dressed in the dark.' Janey snapped her mouth shut, feeling herself go an unbecoming shade of crimson.

But Freddy rounded on Luca. 'That's a horrible thing to

say, Luca!' she squealed. 'Janey worked hard to achieve this look and I think she looks brilliant, for a change. She's very *in the now* tonight. Very *au courant*. How *dare* you.'

It had actually all been Freddy, of course – they were her clothes, after all – but Janey was so furious with Luca's open disapproval that she didn't bother to correct Freddy's false assertion. 'You wouldn't know the first thing about fashion, so, so, drop dead, you j-judgemental beast!' Janey stuttered at the back of Luca's head.

Without missing a beat, Luca shot back, 'If I were to, as you say, drop dead, *signorina*, how far would you be able to walk to your rave in your too-high shoes?'

Of course, being the numero uno ladies' man that he was, he had to have noticed that little detail! Janey fumed, her head about to blow off in sheer temper. It was a weird feeling for her, because she was regarded as the cosmic peacekeeper of Selbourne High. Nothing *ever* got under her skin. Except Luca. For all the *wrong* reasons. She could only manage a gargling noise.

'*Chillax*, you two,' Freddy said, looking from Luca to Janey in open fascination. 'Tonight's supposed to be about Peace, Love, Unity, and Respect, remember? So stop comparing her with your posse of overdressed, busty, blondely botoxed babes, Luca Sarti, because Janey's *one of a kind*.'

Janey just sank down lower in her seat in humiliation. If that was his type, she thought, then it was all utterly hopeless and she might as well give up now.

Nobody spoke another word before the car drew up at the

Piazzale Ugo La Malfa, which was teeming with a diverse cross-section of partygoers. Trippy hippy types, hip-hoppers, face-painted teens wearing DayGlo and clutching glowsticks, d'n'b aficionados, hardstyle trancers, tekheads, plain old weirdos and everything in between. Strobe lights cut the air above the Circus Maximus, the night sky illuminated with eerie giant images and pulsing with a mingled roar of competing beats. The entire scene was set off by the immense scale of the Circus Maximus itself, which was set in a valley between some of the highest hills of Rome and littered with stone ruins that marked where the stadium had once stood.

Too upset with Luca to even say goodbye, Janey flung herself out of the car as Freddy held a brief exchange with Luca in Italian before slamming the door. He drove away without a backward glance.

Janey was so distressed by Luca's attack on her appearance that she could barely breathe. The crowd pressing in on all sides wasn't helping either.

Freddy gave her a hard poke in the ribs to get her attention before pulling her by the wrist into the gigantic throng of partygoers making their way towards the main gate.

'Don't lose me!' she screamed as Janey nodded her understanding. This was *vast*.

Despite her misery, her pulse began to race.

Freddy retrieved two passes clipped to lanyards out of her wristlet clutch before they got to the main entryway, and jammed one over Janey's head just as they surged through the turnstiles with what felt like a thousand other people.

People were squealing and crying out in the crush and, without warning, Janey couldn't see Freddy *anywhere*. She was through, and surrounded by thousands of revellers, all freeforming to their music of choice. The night was a blur of pounding music, and glowsticking, and bodies in motion. It was *amazing*.

For a moment, Janey just stood and took it all in. Then she pivoted around, searching for any sign of Freddy and the Goa trance arena. It didn't help that she didn't know what Goa trance music was supposed to sound like, but at least she had a vague idea where Freddy and her friends were likely to be hanging out. Janey could see six main stages or arenas – it wouldn't be too hard to narrow down which one was playing the right sound.

She began moving towards the nearest arena in her uncomfortable heels, through a sea of shifting dancers. 'Why did I let Freddy convince me to wear these ridiculous things?' she muttered ruefully as she dodged a half-naked guy covered in body paint.

'Eh, English girl,' a young Italian guy roared at her a moment later as he slipped a sweaty, heavy arm around her neck, 'you want be friends?'

'No thanks!' Janey yelled back, ducking out from under his arm and backing away. The guy blew her a wobbly, no-hard-feelings kind of kiss before trying the same move on another passing female.

Janey wrinkled her nose and kept moving towards the nearest sound stage, which was surrounded by enormous speakers and throwing up strobe lights and laser beams in technicolour. The music was so loud and so fast that the first dancer she grabbed onto to try and figure out where she was just shook his head and pointed at his ears.

She backed away and prodded someone else in the arm. 'Goa trance?' she screamed at a young woman who was crazily glowsticking figure eights in the air. The beat pounded through Janey's body.

'Gabber!' the young woman bellowed in Janey's ear before melting away.

The next partygoer Janey tried to ask shook his head in time to the furious beat and screamed the same thing. Janey figured it had to be the style of music.

As the night wore on, Janey began to feel overwhelmed by the swelling, bellowing crowd and the pulsing, deafening music that came from every direction and seemed to vibrate right through her body. She worked her way around every sound stage and realised that Freddy's friends must have given her the wrong information about where to meet, because the next arena offered d'n'b, another happy hardcore, the fourth psy-trance, the fifth chemical break and the last ambient space music, which sounded less like music and more like the soundtrack to a dopey sci-fi movie. The dancers at the last stage were so relaxed and trippy that Janey felt like she'd been grabbed and hugged by almost everyone there. Frustratingly, no one she'd asked seemed to know what Goa trance was.

Exhausted and dispirited, she plunged through a curtained doorway into a designated chill-out room – a large, dimly lit marquee that had been erected roughly midway between the two largest sound stages. Settling onto a low divan next to a sleeping girl and a couple with their arms wrapped around each other, Janey closed her eyes and let the gentle lounge music mix just wash over her. It felt like she'd been embracing a million different people for hours, half of whom had wanted to take her home! She wondered whether Freddy was all right and thought momentarily, with regret, that she wouldn't get to dance with Brandon tonight because it was probably time to return to Celia's. She was never going to find Freddy and her friends now; it seemed really late and if anything, the crowd had grown a whole lot bigger. Without her phone or her watch, Janey couldn't really be sure what the time was and she didn't want to risk staying out past two.

As Janey bent down to take her shoes briefly off her aching, blistered feet, someone draped a muscular arm around her waist from behind, pulling her close. The stranger slurred something crude-sounding in Italian, to which Janey disgustedly replied, 'Non capisco! I don't understand.' She tried to wriggle free of the man's tight hold, but he was really strong, and (double ick!) really hairy to boot. Janey had had enough of strange guys coming up and touching her that night to last a lifetime. Most had been harmless, but there was something about this guy that shrieked *super creepy*. She struggled harder.

Instead of letting her go, the man crushed Janey even closer to him and purred into her hair, 'Lei vuole X? The ecstasy?

You want?' He shook a bag of bright pills just by her ear. Janey felt a stab of real fear.

'It's about control, and about self-respect,' her mother had said when the subject of drugs had come up at home, while they'd been watching something together. Lydia had been a cool mum who never lectured her daughter. 'I'm never going to try and *stop* you doing anything,' she had added. 'But always be aware that things can turn in an instant. And some things can never be undone. Don't stuff your life up over one cheap thrill, that's all I'm saying.'

Janey remembered this now and shook her head, struggling to escape the man's embrace. But he laughed harshly and tried to pull her face around for a kiss. Twisting her head away, she lost her balance as he let go of her, and fell into an untidy heap of arms and legs on the ground. A couple of people looked up disinterestedly before returning to their conversations. Janey was glad that in the moodily lit space, no one could see the tears in her eyes.

The dealer laughed as Janey struggled to her feet, badly shaken. She batted her way furiously out of the marquee, holding her borrowed heels.

Hours after she and Freddy had been separated, Janey – on the verge of tears – had had enough. Her feet hurt, her head hurt, she'd been pawed at by a tonne of strangers, she'd had to fight off a creepy drug dealer and, ironically, had never felt so alone in all her life. The night that had started so promisingly had become a nightmare. She just wanted it to be over.

Without looking back, she limped barefooted towards the Piazzale Ugo La Malfa and the first taxicab she could flag down.

Celia, arms crossed and wearing a wrap over her nightgown, launched herself at Janey as soon as she let herself into the apartment. 'You're late! *And* you look like a *train wreck*. Do you know how *worried* I've been about you?'

Janey glanced at the hallway clock, which read 2.49 a.m., and her insides turned to ice. 'I'm really sorry,' she mumbled, pushing hair out of her eyes, 'but I lost Freddy. Looked for her all night. No watch.' It seemed too hard to put everything she'd gone through into words.

'You could have called her!' Celia hissed. Janey remained miserably silent. Freddy had told her mother they were carrying mobiles; telling Celia that Freddy had lied right from the start was probably a sure-fire way of *not* improving Celia's mood.

'But you didn't, did you, because you had other plans!' Celia accused. 'Freddy told me you got through the turnstiles together but you pretty much ditched her straight away for the first stoner you saw!'

Janey froze. How could Freddy have told her *that* unless she was home already?

Celia nodded as the realisation dawned in Janey's eyes. 'She said she spent the rest of the night looking for you but gave up and came home early when she realised how late it was, and how hopeless it would be trying to find you in a crowd of twenty thousand people! She was so exhausted, she went straight to bed.' Celia pointed at Freddy's bedroom door.

Janey was struggling to process what Celia was saying. 'That's not true!' she insisted. 'I lost sight of *her*. And some guy *did* put his arm around me but I pushed him away. She probably saw him do it and misunderstood. I've been looking for Freddy for *hours*, just like she's been looking for *me*.'

'Which explains why you've got bruise marks on your arms and knees, and lipstick smeared across your face,' Celia retorted. 'I can't believe how *wrong* I've been about you, Jane! I don't need more issues, not with *you* too. You're new to this city, and you're in my care. A thousand horrible things could've happened to you. Clean yourself up and go to bed. We'll talk about this in the morning.'

Celia disappeared into her bedroom and shut the door. Entering her own bedroom, Janey took one look at her bedraggled reflection in the wardrobe mirrors and burst into tears. She'd never broken curfew before, *ever*, and then as soon as she met the long-lost family she so wanted to impress and keep in her life, she looked like a complete flake!

The one person who could've made her feel better about the whole fiasco – her mum – was beyond reach. The thought just made Janey cry harder. Lydia would've just laughed about the misunderstandings. *And* she would've been proud of how Janey had stood up for herself against that drug-dealing gorilla in the chill-out room.

The thought that Celia's opinion of her had surely sunk only made Janey feel more lonely and lost than ever. Until it dawned on her several moments later, as she lay looking at the ornate ceiling through a teary haze, that she *did* have someone she could pour her heart out to.

Janey crept down the hall to the study, closed the door and switched on the desk lamp beside the computer. She logged in via her aunt's login screen. 'Please be there,' she pleaded under her breath. It was around eleven o'clock on Saturday morning back home. One of them *had* to be online.

She scanned the desktop icons and brought up the Skype welcome screen. She typed in her Skype name and password and pulled up her contacts list. Only Gabs was online.

Janey picked up the headset lying beside the computer, checked the position of the webcam above the monitor and hit the start button on the screen, crossing her fingers that everything would work.

As Gabs's wonderfully familiar features sprang into focus, Janey kept her voice low. 'Hey, Gabs. It's so good to see you. You don't know *how* good.'

'What happened to your *face*, Janes?' Gabs exclaimed from her perch in front of her grandma's computer. 'Are you wearing *leopard print*?'

Janey started crying again, making what remained of her make-up run even more. Her story tumbled out in short bursts as she sniffed and hiccupped.

'*Why* would Freddy say that?' Gabs burst out after she'd managed to piece together Janey's night.

Feeling a little calmer, Janey sighed. 'Maybe she really did think I'd ditched her for that guy, I don't know. It was dark. He just grabbed me, plus he was half naked. It would've looked pretty bad. You can't blame Freddy – she'd bent over backwards to help me get party-hearty all day, which I was pretty amazed about! All I know is that Celia now thinks I'm some kind of skank.' Janey hadn't known it was possible to feel so homesick, or so low.

Gabs frowned. 'That is the *wrongest* thing I've ever heard in my life! Whatever the opposite of a skank is, you're it. Now get some sleep. I'll update the others.'

'It's okay,' Janey yawned. 'I'll do it via MySpace before I go to bed. I want to get my impressions down while they're still fresh. Leaving aside the Goa trance fiasco, the whole thing *was* a pretty surreal experience. Parts of it were mind-blowing.'

'Just keep us posted,' Gabs replied in a troubled voice. 'And stay out of Celia's way for a while until she cools off. I'm sure it was all a misunderstanding and you guys will laugh about it tomorrow.'

'I will,' Janey promised. 'I'll log on daily – once the coast is clear.'

'And stay away from leopard print,' said Gabs with a grin. 'It does *nothing* for you!'

Centro Storico

When Janey opened her eyes the next morning, everything that had happened the night before flooded back in reverse order.

She grinned as she remembered Gabs's parting words on Skype, winced as she recalled the argument with Celia, and gave a mental shudder as she remembered her horrible encounter with the sleazy drug dealer. She'd been lucky to get off so lightly.

Then Janey smiled as she recalled how the strobes had lit up the sky over the Circus Maximus. Parts of the night *had* been beautiful, and filled with happy strangers. And she never would've experienced any of it if she hadn't gone. But one more thing made her stomach flip over, and that was the memory of Luca's disdain.

Luca.

Janey's mouth turned down. She'd been a huge chump for even letting the guy get under her skin.

Busty blondes! she thought to herself. *Ha!* She definitely wasn't going to be one of *those* when she grew up.

Janey crawled out of bed, still wearing the things she'd gone out in the night before.

As she stumbled out of her bedroom to the kitchen, Janey mentally rehearsed the kinds of casual, breezy things to say to an aunt who thinks you're some kind of subterranean *troll*, and to a glamour-puss cousin who believes you'd hook up with the first stranger who walks by. So she was *very* relieved to find the kitchen empty of all life, apart from a note from Celia that read:

> *Sorry, overreacted.*
> *Worried as hell. Had to get to work early.*
> *Deadlines. Talk tonight?*
> *Celia xx*

Janey binned the note and made herself a coffee before heading back to her room to survey the damage, studying herself in the mirrored doors of her built-in robe.

Celia had been right. She *had* come home looking like a train wreck. And she'd been so exhausted that she'd climbed straight into bed after her late-night computer bender, still wearing full war paint and the improbable outfit that Freddy had somehow brainwashed her into wearing.

'You look like a clown,' said Janey to her own reflection.

'No wonder he thinks you're a joke!'

Her eye make-up was smeared down her cheeks and looked like a surrealist painting, while her lipstick had migrated across the lower half of her face. The paleness of her freckly skin highlighted several bad bruises on her arms and legs. And in the morning sunlight, her red mini and loud empire-line top were just Eurotrash awful. Sure, it was a look that Kate Moss might've pulled off, but on Janey, it was just *bad*.

Disgusted with herself, Janey dragged off Freddy's clothes, scrubbed her face and had a long shower. Back in her bedroom, she changed into the comfy grey T-dress and pulled her hair back into a low side ponytail.

'That's better,' she said out loud, opting for a little light coverage to hide the huge dark circles under her eyes. 'Now, if we could try and have a nice, humiliation-free day today, that would be just fabulous.' She gave her reflection a tired, lopsided grin.

Janey was just getting her guidebooks out of her backpack when her mobile phone rang, the one that Celia had given her two days before. In the stillness of the apartment, the shrill and unfamiliar ringtone froze Janey in her tracks. She dug the phone out.

Luca (mobile).

She relaxed and broke into a broad smile, until she remembered that Luca had thought her responsible for the way she'd looked last night. So her 'Ciao, Luca,' was a little uncertain.

'Ciao, cara,' Luca replied in his familiar, deep drawl.

Note to self, thought Janey as her stomach swooped, then hastily righted itself. *Look up what* that *means!*

They both started talking at once.

'I shouldn't have . . .' started Janey.

'You looked . . .' Luca began.

'You first,' said Janey. 'And I didn't mean to call you a beast. You were right. I did look really, really terrible.'

'Not terrible,' Luca replied amusedly. 'Just like the B-grade movie star! Though I could 'ave put it better.'

'You could have,' Janey laughed ruefully. 'But you're also too *kind*. I looked thoroughly *F*-grade. Now did you, um, mean to call me? Celia's not home, if that's who you're looking for.'

Because there has to be a logical explanation for why we're talking, thought Janey wryly.

'Certo,' Luca responded. 'I am indeed calling you. It is my, how do you Australians say, "off" day? And my many girlfriends, they are busy, so . . . you are free for a little walking?'

Janey's mouth quirked up as she tried to keep the astonishment out of her voice. 'I am most assuredly free for a little walking.' The day suddenly looked very much the opposite of 'off'. She tossed the guidebooks back into her daypack as Luca rang off, promising to be there in fifteen minutes.

Pretty soon, the buzzer sounded and Janey checked her reflection critically one more time before bounding out of the apartment and out through the villa's grand front entrance. Luca was leaning up against the low brick wall that separated the villa's immaculate formal gardens from the street, with his hands in his pockets. The smile that lit up his eyes as soon as he spotted Janey did something funny to her breathing. *He really does seem happy to see me!* she thought wonderingly.

Of course, he was also looking totally crush-worthy in a sleek, black, open-necked shirt with the shirt sleeves rolled up each tanned forearm, worn jeans with hems of just the right degree of frayed-ness, and black leather slides. Janey had to stop a huge, goofy grin from breaking out all over her face.

'Come sta, signorina?' Luca smiled as he pushed away from the front wall and slid his blue-tinted aviators onto his nose. He looked down at Janey's feet, which she presented for his inspection, telling herself fiercely not to question her luck or pry about those other (grrrr!) *girlfriends*.

'Flats – no more "too-high-shoes",' she grinned, recalling Luca's words from the night before. 'Although I can't do much about my too-big feet. And no more "signorina" from now on, as Freddy ordered. It's just Janey.'

Luca smiled and shrugged before taking one of Janey's hands in his, as if it were the most natural thing in the world. *To him, maybe!* thought Janey, telling herself firmly not to get too excited, because he probably did this with everybody. She tried hard to act normal and not hyperventilate all over the place. And with that, began one of the most perfect days of her life.

They started with coffee and pastries at a dimly lit little café just north of the Stazione Centrale Roma Termini, where the few locals who were about on this hot, sleepy Sunday morning took their breakfast standing up as they browsed through the morning's papers.

'Just keep walking,' Luca insisted laughingly when Janey queried where they were off to next. 'We have much to see.' He wrapped his fingers through hers again and they were off on a day-long magical mystery tour that served up a mind-boggling mix of ancient wonders, awe-inspiring window-shopping and people-watching opportunities and – Luca having read Janey well – *plenty* of pit stops for eating.

'This granita is an absolute godsend,' sighed Janey as they sat at a tiny, marble-topped table in one of the narrow corridors packed with portraits and landscapes that the Antico Caffè Greco – located in the heart of Rome's designer shopping district – was world-famous for. They'd been criss-crossing the ancient city centre for hours already and had seen so many frescoed churches, galleries, museums and public buildings that Janey had run out of space on her camera's memory card. It was *stuffed* with photos of obscure obelisks, ceremonial arches, columns commemorating long-forgotten battles, carved marble angels by the score and, of course, photos of Janey clowning around Rome's many fountains. Luca had ducked out of the frame with a smiling shake of his head the few times Janey had tried to capture him doing the same.

Luca threw his head back now and laughed. He looked coolly out of place among the flushed and badly dressed tourists thronging the almost 250-year-old former hangout of poets, lovers, kings, composers and artists. Janey had spent most of the afternoon pigging out on what Luca had decreed the world's best tartufo, gelato, piadina, antipasto and bruschetta. 'Miracolo!' he said. 'That there is room in your stomach, even for that...'

Janey giggled as she scooped up the last of the lemon syrup-infused ice drink with a silver spoon and snaffled the last piece of torrone from the plate that lay between them. 'Me and buffets?' she grinned, popping the sticky-sweet nougat confection into her mouth, 'it's not pretty. Where to now?'

It was almost four, and they'd also managed to name-check the flagship Valentino, Fendi, Armani, Gucci, Versace and D&G stores. Just being with Luca had made her less nervous about breezing through as if she could actually afford anything inside! Janey wasn't sure how much more of the city she could take in, though she was loving it all and not wanting the day to ever end. Though it had been slightly marred by the number of mobile phone calls Luca had had to take. And the vast majority of them *had* been from girls; Janey could tell by the way Luca's eyes softened and his sexy voice suddenly implied that the caller was the most important woman in the world. Each time he hung up, he would apologise, making Janey yearn for a little less impeccable politeness from him. Maybe if she suddenly grew a bust or got, like, a metre of blonde hair extensions, she might have more luck, Janey thought as the phone rang for the umpteenth time.

Though she told herself not to be stupid. *She* was the person he was holding hands with after all. And after their fight last night, today was a gift. She pushed away the niggling thought that Celia would *not* approve.

'Just one more place,' said Luca after the call ended, refusing to elaborate as they walked back out into the hot afternoon sunshine and headed back up the winding streets towards the Via Veneto, the place that Janey had called Em from the other day, centre of all things Fellini. 'To reach the villa, we must pass it.'

They dashed across the always psychotically busy Piazza Barberini together towards yet another church – located at the foot of the Via Veneto – which stood in stark contrast to the functional-looking government buildings, fancy hotels, sports car showrooms and bus stops that surrounded it on all sides.

Luca said quietly, 'Santa Maria della Concezione dei Cappuccini. Built in 1626 by Cardinal Antonio Barberini. It is one of our city's greatest secrets. All the people I drive, for the embassy, this they *always* want to see.'

Janey looked up at the dirty brick and plaster façade of the unremarkable-looking church and wrinkled her forehead. Perhaps it was something to do with . . . coffee?

'Um,' she said, pushing her fringe out of her eyes, 'is there a must-see fresco in there? Because I'm all out of memory.' She dangled her camera.

Luca smiled. 'The fratelli, the Capuchin friars, they do not allow the pictures, in any case. Your eyes, they are enough.'

He ushered her up the front steps and led her through the church towards a man dressed in plain religious robes, who Janey realised must be a friar.

'You ready?' Luca asked, placing a donation into the friar's bowl for the two of them. Janey smiled her assent, wondering what this simple-looking building could possibly house that made it so famous. Strangely, they had the building almost to themselves, for the heat of the day had driven the crowds of tourists to seek the cool of nearby department stores, gelaterias and tearooms.

They followed the friar as he led them beneath the church and in through a series of barred iron gates.

Janey drew in a shocked breath. *She didn't believe what she was seeing*.

It was a six-roomed crypt. And five of the rooms were decorated, floor to ceiling, with human bones and skulls that had been used to form shapes, patterns and Christian symbols. Here and there full-sized skeletons reposed in Capuchin robes, or were made to resemble the Grim Reaper, complete with scythe.

'It is an ossuary,' Luca murmured as the silent, elderly monk took them from one bone-filled room to another. 'Almost four thousand are here. The Capuchin dead, and also the poor of Rome, who could not find burial elsewhere. It is interesting, no?'

The further they progressed within the dimly lit crypt, the fainter Janey felt. Maybe it was the heat, or the claustrophobic closeness of the place, or even the densely patterned swirls made up of human vertebrae and other bones that marched across the walls and ceilings, but Janey felt herself begin to sway. She was a tender-hearted creature and was the only one, of all her friends, who had to watch the gory parts of horror movies through her fingers. There were even lampshades made out of bones, Janey noted in horror.

'I'm sorry, Luca,' she mumbled suddenly, 'but I think I'm going to be *sick*.'

Luca glanced sharply at her and said something to their guide in rapid Italian before putting an arm around Janey and whisking her back outside. He sat Janey down on the front stairs of the church. It was five minutes before she could bring herself to say anything, her embarrassment was so great.

'I'm sorry,' she said, the colour slowly returning to her face. 'But I'm just a bit *over* death at the moment.'

'No,' Luca replied grimly, 'it is *I* who am sorry. I was not thinking. Sua madre . . .'

Janey shook her head. 'Mum would've thought this was a hoot. Especially the Latin inscription at the exit that says: "What you are, we used to be. What we are, you will be." It's so *true*, and so very clever. But I'm not a very brave person. And it's a hot day. I just needed some air. I guess I'm just tired.'

In fact, the place had reminded Janey all too forcefully of the stark realities of death. A wave of panicky nausea threatened to overwhelm her again and she took several deep breaths to get her emotions under control, hoping she wouldn't throw up on Luca's sandals.

'Then we 'ave seen enough today,' he responded. 'And you are very brave, more brave than Federica and her friends, who hid their fear of this place in jokes and foul language that made the Capuchin who was their guide very angry. He asked them to leave.'

Janey gave him a wan smile. When some of her colour had returned, Luca hauled her gently to her feet and took one hand again in his, tucking it into the crook of his elbow.

They wound their way slowly back up the Via Veneto, stopping for one more watermelon granita, which succeeded in banishing the last of Janey's melancholy mood. When they finally reached Celia's villa, Luca left Janey at the front entrance with a gentle kiss on the forehead. And she closed her eyes for a moment as he walked briskly away without a backward look, her mouth a gentle, happy curve.

Freddy was home and using the computer in the study as Janey let herself in.

'Hi Freddy,' Janey called as she walked past the room where Freddy sat shrieking into the screen in Italian, the headset and webcam on.

Freddy waved gaily before nudging the door shut with one foot.

Two hours later and Janey – showered and dressed for ages and wondering whether she should attempt to make dinner for her hosts or suggest an outing – overheard a heated discussion in Italian in the hallway just outside her room. *Celia must be back*, Janey thought, as she opened her bedroom door. Her aunt must have been waylaid on embassy business. Plus, they ate late here. She pinned a smile on her face, determined to clear the air with her aunt about why she'd returned so late from the rave. She was sure they would be laughing about it in no time.

'Hi!' Janey said, as she looked from Celia's thunderous expression to Freddy's worried one and wondered why her cousin suddenly murmured, 'Good luck!' before grabbing her handbag and flying out of the apartment.

'Did I not make it *clear*,' began Celia, as she paced away from Janey and down the hall towards to the formal sitting room, 'that you are to stay away from Luca Sarti, except in the case of a dire emergency?'

Janey's smile faltered as she followed her aunt. 'Um, he asked me out for coffee this morning and we ended up doing a little sight-seeing. That's all.'

'That's *all*?' Celia exclaimed, tossing her briefcase, handbag and tailored jacket down carelessly on the nearest divan before turning and planting her hands on her hips.

Janey nodded uncertainly.

Celia looked slightly incredulous. 'And when does "sight-seeing" include you *kissing* Luca on the front steps *of this villa*, in full sight of the families of most of my closest friends and colleagues *in this city*? Steven Edwards in 1B saw the two of you on his way out when you got back from doing God knows what today. He assumed you were Luca's latest squeeze! I assured him you most certainly were *not* and clarified that you were my sixteen-year-old niece. You've been alone together for *hours*! You're way too young to get involved with someone like him. I don't want you to get hurt or get yourself into trouble. Don't make me bring this up with him! Luca Sarti is off-limits in the romance department. Do I make myself clear? *Again*?'

Janey nodded shakily, knowing Celia had hopelessly misread an entirely innocent situation. *Again*.

'Maybe this was all a bad idea,' said Celia, lowering her voice. 'Maybe I should just put you back on a plane to Australia before you make a mistake like...' She stopped herself before she said anything more hurtful and added over her shoulder as she walked away, 'I'll just be in the kitchen fixing us something simple to eat, unless you have other plans...'

The implication was clear. Her aunt had been about to say, 'Before you make a mistake like... your *mother* did.'

Janey blinked hard before spinning on her heel and retreating to the study in order to log on to her MySpace page. She needed to process and share her incredible day. For some reason, her aunt was determined to believe the worst about her. Her friends, wherever they were, would know what to say to make her feel better. Tearily, she began to blog.

MYBLOG

'Well, friends and citizens of Cyberia, it's been just another day of Heaven and Hell in the Eternal City. Here's the story so far...'

Trastevere

Janey stayed in the study busily uploading photos and responding to concerned queries from her online buddies long after Freddy had returned to the apartment, and both she and Celia had retired to their bedrooms. Earlier, Celia had slipped into the study with a dinner tray of cured meats, chargrilled vegetables and cheeses for Janey, but they hadn't really spoken again because Celia had had to take an important call almost immediately.

'Call me tomorrow?' she'd told Janey distractedly – back in work mode – as she hurried out of the study. Janey had nodded and whispered her thanks, but she hadn't looked up, not wanting her aunt to see how upset she was. Things were still up in the air between them, and it bothered Janey a *lot*, especially since she'd travelled halfway around the world to meet the only family she had left and silly misunderstandings were threatening to ruin everything. She *hated* conflict.

But it felt great reconnecting with her vast network of friends from around the world, most of whom could see she needed cheering up, and *fast*. Postings went up faster than she could answer them, and after a while, Janey stopped crying as she recounted the more spectacular parts of her day with Luca.

	Sounds like a hottie	
		Razzle Girl

	White hot!	
	Xtreme NV.	*Minxie10*

	Keep urself nice! ;)	
		Bille88

Unfortunately, the three people Janey wanted to hear from the most weren't online. It was Sunday morning back home and they were probably all sleeping in. But Janey knew that before too long, Em, Gabs and Ness would catch up on her latest blog and demand a Skype conference call or something. It was the way the four of them dealt with a crisis when they weren't all able to be physically present in the one place for each other.

It was nice to know that people cared, thought Janey tiredly, as she finally logged out around one in the morning.

When she finally got to bed, she was so exhausted that she fell asleep straight away, and slept deeply without dreaming.

With a shock, she woke to find it was almost one o'clock on Monday afternoon.

Celia was probably at work and, Janey noted as she stumbled down the hallway, Freddy was still asleep in her bedroom after yet another late night with her glamorous BFFs and BBFs. Brandon was right when he'd described her cousin, Janey mused with a yawn. She *could* be a little full-on.

Janey headed back to the study with a coffee, eager to see whether her three besties had caught her latest blog. It had been *so* long since she'd spoken with Ness! Janey owed her *big time* for playing fairy godmother and totally accentuating her positives.

She logged back in to her MySpace page, almost spilling coffee down her front in excitement. The very latest posting was from Em, from about six hours before.

 We'll wait to hear from u (skype!!!) either 11.30 am or 11.30 pm (wont get to sleep in with this one, but wont hold it against u!) Monday ur time. Pls b there?

The Divine Miss Em

Thanks to Janey's cyber bender the night before, she'd missed the first of the appointed rendezvous times, but there was only about ten hours to kill before the next one. And boy, did she have a lot of stuff to tell her best mates face to face that no amount of blogging could even begin to convey!

Feeling a lot calmer than she had the night before, Janey scrolled back down to the last comment she'd looked at and started reading upwards. Distracted by playing around with the background wallpaper on her page, it took her a while to notice that a new comment had been posted, just above Em's.

Immediately, she felt a chill run up her spine.

 Hey loser. Don't read so much into 1 lousy kiss, will ya?   *Fellini*

Without warning, Fellini and his chillingly familiar car crash avatar had popped up again. *In real time*.

Janey stared at the posting in horror. She hadn't said anything about any kiss in her latest blog about Rome. It had been something so private, and so special, that she'd only planned to tell her besties about it.

Janey's mind spun. Who *was* this creep? That guy in 1B whom she'd never even met? She refused to believe it could be Luca, slamming the lid on that traitorous thought, though a tiny, rational part of her mind insisted that it *could* be. She forced her shaking hands into action.

Who's the loser? U following me?

            x X Janey G X x

There was a long pause. Janey refreshed her page a few times. When nothing new appeared, she thought, with relief, that maybe Fellini was logging out. But one click later, she saw:

Lets just say I *know* what u did yesterday
& Im keeping MY I on U.   *Fellini*

Janey leapt away from the screen as if someone had doused her with a bucket of iced water. She scanned the study as if Fellini had somehow managed to plant a camera in there with her.

She sat back down slowly. Her stomach did a double backflip when she refeshed her page again and read:

Every breath U take every move U make baby.   *Fellini*

Chilled to the core, Janey hurriedly shut down. She threw on the orange tank and white shorts, grabbed her rucksack and fled into another bright, hot and lazy Roman afternoon feeling as if Fellini was right behind her and breathing down her neck.

Almost unconsciously, Janey headed as far away from her aunt's villa in an unfamiliar direction, wanting to lose herself in some obscure but busy corner of town where Fellini couldn't *possibly* be.

So she cut through the historical centre of Rome, heading across the River Tiber to a district called Trastevere.

Trastevere didn't have a whole lot of obvious tourist destinations, but her guidebook indicated it was still one of the most happening areas of Rome. It was a picture-book old quarter of the city where *real* Romans still lived, packed with bars, cafés, hip shopping spots, and atmospheric public squares. It was also riddled with narrow cobbled streets, making it a great place to get lost in the crowd, which was exactly what Janey needed. To lose that horrible feeling of being watched by unseen eyes. She needed time to just think and *chill*.

By the time she crossed the Ponte Sisto into Trastevere, the breezy outfit she'd thrown on just over an hour before was plastered to her willowy frame but her usual positivity had returned. As she looked around, she saw hundreds of people of almost as many nationalities and Janey could feel herself relaxing a little. Fellini – whoever he was – couldn't possibly *be* here in Rome actually tailing her around. He was probably some spotty twelve-year-old moron from Florida or somewhere.

Janey followed the swell of people ducking into and out of the medieval churches, marvelling at the ancient mosaics and astonishing domes, sculptures and icons that featured on almost every building. In between, she browsed the leather goods stores, specialty paper shops and museums that seemed to occupy every street corner. She kept herself hydrated with slices of fresh watermelon, and one sweet and icy grattachecca after another.

Trastevere was the perfect antidote to the poisonous situations she'd been experiencing with her aunt. The streets were crooked and crowded with ancient apartment buildings and villas that seemed to lean into one another. High above her head, the lines of colourful washing that stretched across from building to building just added to the festive air of the place. Through the shutter-framed windows of their abodes, Romans could be glimpsed talking on the telephone, preparing food, chasing their children and just generally going about their business.

Family's so important, Janey thought, determined to try and explain her side of the story to Celia the next chance she got. Celia really seemed to care about her, though she was willing to leap to the most awful conclusions about her character! And that hurt. A lot.

After an overload of ancient history, Janey headed for the busy café scene that centred on the Piazza di Santa Maria in Trastevere, its radiating laneways crowded with eateries. She'd just ordered a late afternoon tea at the bustling Sabatini, and was enjoying her coffee, when her mobile phone buzzed loudly. Janey dug through her bag with a smile on her face, thinking it had to be Luca texting to find out how her day had been. But she recoiled as she read the message in her inbox and suddenly felt ill.

> Nver liked Trastevere in
> summer. Too many tourists,
> dont u think?

With a chill, she realised immediately who the text was from. Fellini!

The accompanying mobile number was a local Italian number that Janey didn't recognise. It didn't tally with any of the pre-programmed numbers in her phone for Celia, Luca, Freddy or Brandon. Signalling frantically to her waiter, Janey hastily cancelled her food order, fumbled out the right amount of change for the coffee and almost ran out of the piazza. As she hurried back towards the Ponte Sisto, she searched the faces of the people passing, wondering fearfully if any of them might be *him*. Because how would he know where she was unless *he* was somewhere nearby?

Once she'd crossed back over the bridge, she picked up her pace, because to get back to the Via Veneto area of Rome – which was the closest area of the old city to Celia's apartment – she still had to cut through the Campo dei Fiori, Piazza della Rotonda and Quirinal districts. Suddenly, her aunt's apartment seemed like a haven she couldn't reach fast enough and she cursed herself for heading out at all that afternoon and foolishly believing Fellini didn't pose a real threat!

She still had almost an hour of walking left when she came across a huge protest going on in the piazza she'd intended to take a short cut through on the Quirinal Hill. There were hundreds of people milling about in the square, holding placards she couldn't decipher. The road blockades and heavy police presence meant that she, as well as about a thousand other tourists, was being redirected through surrounding laneways. Janey realised with frustration that this would take her well out of her way and back into the Piazza di Spagna tourist district, a place choked with people and impossibly hilly.

If I don't see another hill in this lifetime, thought Janey – trying to puzzle out where she'd ended up, with the help of her guidebook – *that would be too soon.*

She found herself shuffling slowly up a street whose name she didn't know, which was crawling with overheated and annoyed tourists and locals. She almost screamed out loud when someone grabbed at the back of her tank top.

'Sorry! Tripped,' said a woman in an English accent, before letting go of her hold on Janey.

Janey threw the woman a tight smile and threaded her way quickly to another part of the slowly moving throng, just in case she wasn't someone fully random and harmless. Janey had just stopped by a newsvendor's booth to take her sunglasses off and put her guidebook away when she saw something on a nearby side street – one that cut across the lane she was on – that sent a thrill of sudden irrational fear up her spine.

She saw *Luca*, in the embassy car, tooting his horn at the passing press of people, who wouldn't let him through.

Janey, feeling chilled, watched as Luca finally slid the vehicle through a break in the crowd. He hadn't even looked her way or shown any sign that he knew she was there, but it had to be the weirdest, most unbelievable coincidence that both of them were in this obscure corner of the city *at the same time*.

With a pounding heart, Janey pushed her way back into the mass of people slowly making their way up the street, weaving her way forward as fast as she could. She was usually the politest person around – one who'd rather hang back than act pushy – but seeing Luca out here had had the impact of an electric shock. It was suddenly even more vital to get back to Celia's as quickly as possible.

But as Janey was finally pushed out into the Piazza di Spagna with a torrent of other people, she noticed Freddy's friend Brandon coming out of the nearby Burberry store, carrying a loaded shopping bag.

Janey stopped in her tracks as though she'd been hit by lightning. What were the chances of seeing someone *else* she knew in Rome within the space of such a short time? She looked about in panic for somewhere to hide. It was suddenly really important that he not see her.

She abruptly changed direction and made for a leather goods shop back in the direction she'd just come from. Brandon didn't seem to have seen her, she thought wildly. So if he *didn't* follow her into the store, he couldn't possibly be the malevolent presence that had been following her around Rome all afternoon. If he *did* find her, well, he might be the one behind that text message!

Janey scrambled into the ritzy showroom of Sermoneta Gloves, despairing of ever reaching Celia's. The shop was deserted at this hour of the day because the thermostat was probably pushing forty degrees outside and no one in their right mind was looking at buying fur-lined leather gloves right now, but it was the closest place to hide.

She headed straight for a display at the back of the store that was packed with hand-made luxury golf gloves and hovered there, looking nervously out the front windows.

The elegant saleswoman started to say, 'May I help—' when Janey gave a small shriek and hissed, 'Is there a back entrance I can use?'

The woman shook her head in confusion as, like a heat-seeking missile, Brandon's head of wind-ruffled blond hair could be seen bobbing up the main staircase to the showroom. He'd *found* her.

Janey just stared as Brandon strolled into the glove shop as if he did this every day, and said amusedly, 'Janey Gordon! It *is* you. If I didn't know any better I'd say you were trying to hide from me. You changed direction like one of those ducks you see in a carnival shooting parlour.'

Janey just gaped at him. *Ducks?*

He put his arm through hers and led her out of the store, when something inside Janey seemed to snap and she pushed him away before spinning on her heel to run.

'Janey!' Brandon said, catching at her arm. 'What on earth's the matter? Aren't you glad to see me?'

Janey couldn't meet his eyes. She was so freaked by

everything, she needed to get away.

'L-look,' she stammered in a strained voice, 'this might sound kind of crazy, but there is some kind of, of... *cyber stalker* trying to do a number on me today, and in case it's you (sorry, but it very well could be), I'd really like to get back to Freddy's place now, so if you don't mind...'

Brandon's expression was one of baffled astonishment.

'Don't take it the wrong way, Brandon, but I'm trying to shake you off and you're not even remotely co-operating. So if you go that way,' Janey waved him back in the direction of the swanky designer stores on the Via Condotti, 'and I go that way,' she pointed up the seemingly endless marble steps that led away from the Piazza di Spagna towards the Villa Borghese gardens and home, 'that would be a *huge* load off my mind.'

Brandon led her, protesting, towards the Spanish Steps that gave the piazza its name.

'Sit down,' he ordered. 'And tell me exactly what you mean by *cyber stalker*. You lost me right about there.'

Janey slumped in sudden exhaustion, her backpack between her feet as Brandon settled beside her. 'It would be easier to just show you,' she said slowly. She wasn't sure if she could trust him, but maybe just showing him Fellini's message would tell her whether or not Brandon knew anything about it. She was a pretty good reader of people.

Janey dug around in her backpack for the Italian mobile phone that Celia had given her, when it buzzed again, indicating another text was coming through. She dropped the pack as if it was composed of live coals and said shakily, '*You* do it.

It's probably that creep Fellini again.'

Brandon took the bag out of Janey's hands with a look of confusion and retrieved her mobile. Janey took the key lock off and Brandon held the phone up as both of them read the new text.

> He's cute. But dont get
> your hopes up.

Brandon's eyebrows shot up. Janey turned milk white.

'Okay,' said Brandon. 'Start from the beginning.'

The whole weird saga of her day spilled forth. It was a relief to tell someone who actually seemed to care and wanted to hear her out. Celia didn't even seem to have enough time to do that.

'Who *is* this guy?' said Brandon. He scrolled through the inbox to find the earlier message and read that as well, frowning.

'I don't know *who* he is,' Janey said, 'but he's been on my case since Australia, posting freaky comments on my MySpace, and now this. I thought at first it was someone from the rave the other night, or that it was *you*,' Janey laughed shakily as Brandon frowned again and re-read the two messages. 'And then I thought, for a split second, that it might even be Luca. As if!' Her voice was a little hysterical.

She told Brandon about seeing Luca in a part of town she hadn't expected to be in, and certainly hadn't expected to see *him* in. Brandon's look of concern deepened.

'Well,' he replied slowly. 'That may not be the crazy idea you think it is. Didn't you say Fellini's avatar was a black luxury sedan? Does it look anything like the car Luca drives?'

Janey nodded. 'But it *can't* be Luca,' she insisted. 'He took me out yesterday. Why would he do something like this?'

'He's an expert at toying with your emotions, according to Freddy,' Brandon said grimly. 'It's the kind of sick game a guy like him would play. He can't be trusted.'

Janey flinched, recalling that Celia had said something similar.

'And it's not so weird that you ran into me here,' Brandon added. 'Everyone shops here.' Brandon held open his shopping bag, which had the latest Burberry handbag nestled in it, together with a boxed silk scarf in signature nova plaid. Janey's eyes widened at the kind of gift she could never have afforded to give Lydia, no matter how much she deserved it. Then she remembered that Brandon was mega-wealthy and shopping here *was* normal for people like him.

'Mom's birthday,' he shrugged. 'She likes this stuff. So that explains how *I* got here. Luca, however, is another story altogether.'

Janey took in Brandon's explanation silently.

'Why me?' she wailed after a moment. 'Luca and I had a great day together yesterday. We walked all over town. We got along like the proverbial house on fire. The only off note of the whole day was when we visited that awful crypt of human bones on the Via Veneto and he apologised for taking me there . . .'

Brandon's gaze had flown to Janey's sharply when she'd mentioned the crypt. 'It all fits!' he exclaimed. 'The crashed car, Fellini, the Via Veneto, taking you to that gruesome tomb. Don't you see? One minute he's lulling you into a false sense of security, then he's trying to unsettle you the next. He's leaving you clues about who he *really* is. He tried to do exactly the same thing with Freddy when they first met, she tells me.'

It was Janey's turn to look shocked. Luca had pulled the same kind of stunts on her beautiful cousin? Her mind raced.

'He *did* take about a million calls from other girls while we were out together,' she said dismally.

'Look,' said Brandon, 'I'll put you into a cab. After the day you've had, you don't need to be power walking in this heat when all you want to do is get back home.' And he was as good as his word, ordering a cab driver in fluent Italian to get Janey safely and quickly back to Celia's and paying him generously to do it.

Janey sank into the back seat of the taxi and pondered all the new stuff she'd learnt about Luca. Maybe he *was* Fellini. After all, she'd told him almost all there was to know about her life, and it was probably a cinch to send her texts from someone else's number. And the MySpace comments were easy. *Anyone* could do them. Plus, Celia had told her expressly that Luca couldn't be trusted not to break her heart. And he'd been well on his way to at least putting a dent in it. That was, until she'd met Brandon again and he'd set her straight on what a low-life Luca really was!

But why? She'd hoped that maybe, just maybe, they were starting to even be friends, when all the time he'd probably just been trying to mess with her mind . . .

Thank goodness for Brandon, Janey thought, as the taxi drew up in front of her aunt's villa. She made her way shakily up the front steps, thinking that it didn't hurt that he was a *babe*, either.

Gabriel

It was almost eleven-thirty after her freaky day of trying to outrun Fellini's increasingly bizarre attacks.

Janey couldn't wait to see her friends' faces. She didn't think they'd believe the story she was about to lay on them. In the air-conditioned comfort of her bedroom, after a cool shower and the great dinner of vegetarian lasagne that Celia had left in the fridge for her, she almost didn't believe it either.

Imagine, Janey thought with bemusement. *I have a stalker. Like I'm some kind of A-list celeb or something.* It just boggled her mind.

Celia had explained in a note on the fridge that she was stuck entertaining a party of visiting trade delegates that evening, and that Freddy was staying over at Luz's place, so Janey had the apartment, and more importantly, the computer, all to herself.

At eleven-twenty-nine Rome time, Janey Skyped her friends.

Gabs picked up almost instantly and her familiar grin lit up the screen at Janey's end.

'It's *sooooo* good to see you!' Ness squealed from somewhere behind Gabs's left shoulder.

'Ditto to that!' yelled Em, who waved as she crossed the room and moved closer to the monitor, growing bigger in the frame.

The sight of the three of them, clustered around the webcam at Gabs's place, made Janey burst into tears all over again.

'See,' said Gabs, turning to Em and Ness, 'I *told* you she keeps doing that.'

'This is *so* not you, Janes,' Em said with concern. 'What gives?' Ness frowned and nodded in agreement.

It all tumbled out in a weepy, out-of-order diatribe that would've made no sense if it wasn't for her friends' incredible patience at piecing the whole story together.

'It's like some horrible *thriller*,' whispered Ness in consternation after Janey finished her tale of woe.

'Starring *you*,' whistled Em.

'And you *know* what I'm like with horror movies!' Janey gulped, feeling calmer. 'Sorry to lay it all on you guys, but I feel like I've got no one to turn to over here. Freddy seems nice, but she's out all the time with her ritzy pals – and fair enough, she's on her holidays and can't be expected to babysit me – while Celia thinks . . .' Janey blushed, making it clear what Celia thought.

'Anyway.' Janey changed the subject. 'How come you're all together? Isn't it, like, well before eight over there? And I *know* none of you princesses like to rise before noon during the holidays...'

'You're worth more than a little lost beauty sleep to us,' Em responded. 'It was easier for us to prod each other out of our sleeping bags at Gabs's place than to try and drag ourselves to our individual computers at home and hook up a four-way conversation at this hour of the morning! Too logistically taxing, even for *moi*. Plus, we wanted to *see* you. The only way to do that was to all be in the one place.'

'And you guys know technology is so *not* my thing,' Ness added with a laugh. 'I was happy to let someone else fire up the Skype engines and just point myself at the webcam and bat my eyelashes winningly.'

The other three girls giggled. Unless Karl Lagerfeld started making dresses and jewellery out of recycled laptops or something, Ness would continue to shun everything technical apart from her MySpace profile. And even *that*, she had trouble with. She frequently posted blogs that were half finished, by accident. And her wallpaper and photo galleries were pretty half-hearted and blahs-ville for someone so beautiful, with the wardrobe to prove it.

'Maybe you should change your profile to *private*?' suggested Gabs.

'Would that work?' asked Janey, brightening.

'No,' Em interrupted. 'She added Fellini as a *friend*, remember? He can still access her private stuff if he's a "friend".'

Janey's face fell again. 'That's right. I checked Fellini out when this craziness all started, and *his* profile's private. All I know is that he's apparently twenty-one and Italian. Plus, I'm his *only* friend.'

'Eeeuuuuwww,' Gabs exclaimed. 'Now that's creepy.'

A sudden thought made Janey flinch. *Luca* was twenty-one and Italian!

'Well, why don't you remove him?' Ness queried. 'I mean, he's clearly not a friend, is he? He's more like an *anti*-friend.'

'Much as I would love to do that,' said Janey, still bothered by the new link she'd made between Fellini and Luca, 'I kind of want to figure out who he is and what he wants. Remember that old saying, "Keep your friends close and your enemies closer?" He's a bit of a show-off. One day soon, he'll slip up and I'll be onto it. His true and evil identity will be revealed at last and I can tell him to get lost to his face.

'Anyway,' she added sadly, 'it's probably Luca. What Brandon said makes sense. Fellini and Luca seem to have a few too many points in common for my liking. And *why* would an international playboy hottie like him even want to spend a whole day with *me* anyway? It's totally *suss*. He's probably just playing some weird-ass game I don't understand. Apparently he did the same thing to Freddy when they first met, according to Brandon.'

Janey didn't see the quick looks the others shot each other at each mention of Brandon's name.

'Remind me again,' Gabs murmured. 'Brandon is Freddy's underwear model friend?'

Janey laughed. 'No, silly, he's the one I said looked like a walking perfume ad campaign. The all-American, strong-jawed type with wind-swept blond hair.'

'Mmmmmmmmm,' Ness said.

'Well, whatever,' said Em, 'He sounds too good to be true with his white-knight routine.'

Janey frowned and Em added, 'No really! Hear me out. I'm just thinking out loud here. I mean, you've run into the guy *twice* now in Rome. That's one hell of a coincidence strike rate. I mean, remind me, but isn't Rome like a city of, uh, several *million* people?'

Janey shook her head. 'Brandon's been awesome, every time, Em. And super patient and generous. My story's pretty unbelievable, but he still sat through every word and put me in a taxi back to Celia's place when he could've just left me in the Piazza di Spagna – as a spluttering mess, I might add! – and washed his hands of the whole crazy thing! A message came through from Fellini while Brandon was sitting there and he *looked* as stunned as I *felt*. Though I wish my pulse raced around him the way it does around Luca.'

She sighed. 'I'm going to have to go cold turkey where Luca's concerned. He's clearly bad for my health. Especially if he's some psycho freakazoid.'

Em frowned, but didn't push the point.

The four friends talked for almost another hour, Janey asking her buddies for all the goss back home. It felt almost as though they were together again, shooting the breeze in Gabs's room. Except that eventually she had to end the link-up, and the screen showing her friends' smiling faces went abruptly blank.

Uneasy once more, Janey trailed off to bed.

When Celia and Janey met in the hallway the next morning, Celia was friendly, but brisk.

'You forgot to check in with me yesterday,' she said in a mildly accusing tone, as Janey flushed. So much had happened yesterday that it had completely fallen out of her brain!

'No matter,' said Celia more kindly. 'I've arranged for Luca to stop by this morning.' Her eyebrows shot up in surprise as Janey turned pale beneath her lightly developing tan and looked less than pleased at the news. 'He had an unexpected cancellation, and said he could do it. I hope that's okay with you,' Celia continued. 'He'll take you to the Australian Embassy to meet the Ambassador – who's looking forward to meeting you very much – and to tour our building. It's a beautiful place. And you can get Vegemite on toast in the canteen if you're feeling homesick! The Aussie accents you'll hear all around you will be a bonus.'

Celia smiled and rushed off to work, promising to meet up with Janey once she reached the embassy.

Luca was due to ring the security buzzer at ten-thirty. For once, Janey was not looking forward to seeing him at all and was totally unsure about what to wear and how to act. The thought that he was possibly behind the nasty joke that seemed to be unfolding around her made her stomach flip. She'd be stuck in the car with him! What was she supposed to say to a potential stalker? *Hi, how are you? Are you responsible for messing with my head? And could you please* stop*?*

Janey slipped into the wrap dress and ballet flats, deciding on minimal make-up and a low ponytail. When the buzzer sounded she stood up and made for the door as though she was heading to her own execution.

'Ciao bella,' Luca said in his usual heart-stopping way, only today it was heart-stopping for all the wrong reasons. It was suddenly an ordeal to meet his eyes. She just wanted the trip to be over with, before it'd even begun. Janey shook her head when Luca made to open the front passenger door in his usual way, and climbed into the back seat as if she really were a visiting VIP.

'Che?' Luca said, surprised. 'Is anything the matter, Janey?'

'Headache,' Janey lied. 'Don't want to keep the Ambassador waiting, if that's okay. Please just take me there as fast as you can?' She closed her eyes to forestall any more conversation.

Luca shrugged and slid into the driver's seat.

'You are otherwise well?' he began as the car shot out from the kerb. 'You enjoyed our little walk?'

Janey's eyes flicked briefly to his in the mirror, before she looked away.

'I'm fine,' she said. She lapsed into deliberate silence, hoping that he'd take the hint and leave her alone. Half of her was screaming to find out more about him, and the other half was experiencing major trust issues. She hoped the battle of her inner voices wasn't registering on her face.

It couldn't have been, because Luca continued cheerfully, 'My younger sister, Lucia, she and her school friends plan to go to Ostia tomorrow, the beach just outside Roma. She is only a little older than you, and hopes you may join them. She very much wishes to meet you. You will go?'

Under normal circumstances, a trip to the beach, and the opportunity to make exotic new friends her age, would be Janey's idea of heaven. But not now. Not when Janey wasn't sure about Luca's motives for saying or doing anything, where she was concerned.

'Um,' she said. 'I'm kind of busy tomorrow.' She mentally crossed her fingers, hoping he wouldn't ask for details about her plans, because she didn't have any.

'Then mercoledì – Wednesday?' Luca replied. 'She would be most happy to accommodate you.'

Janey shook her head. 'Please tell her molte grazie, but my days are booked up until I leave at the end of next week.' This wasn't at all true, but Janey wasn't sure she wanted to make friends with Luca's sister, even if she did sound lovely and welcoming. It could be another weird trap. It just seemed easier to say no.

She registered Luca's quick frown in the mirror as he changed lanes to avoid a speeding motorcyclist.

Cold turkey, cold turkey, she told herself as she stole a quick, unhappy glance at Luca's back before staring determinedly out a side window. *He seems really nice*, Janey thought to herself, *and you're probably wasting a colossally great chance to get to know him better, you idiot.*

But then again, said her other, more sensible inner voice, *he could be the ultimate weirdo trying to keep tabs on you all the time, in which case you're doing the right thing.*

'I think,' said Luca, 'that you are perhaps – how do you say? – *avoiding me* because I have caused offence in some way. If you will not tell me, I will – what is that English expression? – get to the bottom of things! You cannot escape me so easily, Janey Gordon.'

Janey's eyes shot back to his fearfully, failing to hear the teasing note in Luca's voice with her nerves wound up so tightly. She said nothing, only slid even more firmly into a far corner of the back seat, away from his probing gaze.

Luca said more gently, 'Lucia will be so disappointed! She very much wants to meet the person she calls my "new Australian girlfriend".'

Janey flinched, but did not reply. And minutes later, relief washed over her as they were waved through a boomgate flanked by armed guards. At the front entrance of the building, she sent a nervous smile Luca's way before slipping out of the car and hurrying into the building without looking back.

She gave her name at the reception desk and was handed a visitor's pass. An embassy employee guided her up to the antechamber to the Ambassador's office and politely told her to wait. A moment later, the Ambassador's personal assistant popped her head out of her office and welcomed Janey. Libby was a friendly woman of around Celia's age with a sleek brunette bob, wearing a tailored black pants suit and tortoiseshell Gucci spectacle frames.

'Celia and the Ambassador are still in their nine-thirty meeting,' she apologised. 'And Celia wanted to tour you around personally. She told me to make sure I kept you here. Can I get you anything while you wait?'

Janey smiled and shook her head. 'Have you been working here long?' she asked, staring up at the airy gilded ceilings with their elegant baroque scrollwork.

Libby nodded. 'Gorgeous isn't it?' she said, taking a seat next to Janey. 'I've been with Doug – the Ambassador – and his family since he was second secretary at the London office. I *much* prefer Rome.'

'I've never been to London,' Janey replied with interest. 'What's it like?'

'Centre of the universe,' Libby grinned, 'and boy, does everyone know it! Goes without saying the weather's better here. And the food. The men are pretty easy on the eye too,' she added with a wink.

Libby and Janey chatted for another twenty minutes. When Libby asked how she'd been spending the last few days, Janey reluctantly opened up about the strange things that had been happening to her.

'Almost as if the guy was standing a metre away,' she shuddered, describing the two weirdly specific text messages she'd received only the day before. 'Like he was watching me, no matter where I went or what I was doing.'

'Have you told Celia?' Libby exclaimed. 'You've got to report this, this . . . *cyber bullying* to your aunt. I can't believe you're just dealing with this on your own! We have resources here, we can help you. But you have to tell your aunt everything you've told me!'

Janey sank back a little wearily in her plush armchair. 'I'm not really in Celia's good books at the moment,' she shrugged. 'We've had a couple of small misunderstandings over stupid stuff. *And* she's been really busy, and so have I. We haven't been able to clear the air, and telling her all about my troubles with some mystical Fellini character probably wouldn't help. I'm not sure she'd believe me anyway.'

Libby had to hurry away with a quick apology as the phone suddenly rang in her office, leaving Janey in the luxuriously appointed waiting area.

If she craned her neck, Janey could just make out Libby at her desk, tapping something into her computer while she cradled her handset between her ear and her shoulder.

Janey glanced down at her watch and noticed that it was nearing noon. As if on cue, her stomach rumbled ferociously, and she clutched at it with a tiny laugh, hoping no one had heard. But her laughter died in her throat as the familiar, but unwanted, buzz of her mobile sounded.

It was another text.

She drew the mobile out of her rucksack as if it was a snake, poised to sink its fangs into her hand.

> I'm in the building. Come
> find me? Or I'll find u.
> Either way.

Janey let loose a small shriek and dropped her phone.

Libby paused part-way through her call and looked up. She cupped her hand over the mouthpiece. 'Sorry, Janey! I'll be right with you!' she hissed, before launching back into Italian with her caller.

Janey gingerly picked up her mobile phone and dropped it into her backpack, before scribbling a note on a piece of paper and sliding it under Libby's nose.

> Feeling unwell.
> Will reschedule the tour
> for another day. Soon.
> Nice meeting you!
> Apologise to Celia.

Libby looked up in surprise, halting her phone conversation once more. She called out to Janey to wait, but Janey had already slipped out of the Ambassador's chambers and was clattering down the central staircase to the exits.

On her way out of the embassy grounds, she froze when she saw Luca lounging against the bonnet of the parked car, chatting to another one of the embassy's drivers. *Did that count as being* in *the building?* She panicked. Was he lying in wait for her? Hadn't Luca himself only just said that she couldn't escape him so easily?

Pretending she hadn't seen him, Janey put her head down

and hurried on.

But she could hear Luca's voice behind her, calling out to her to wait!

Janey lost her head completely and scrambled out of the embassy grounds. She climbed onto a nearby bus that was letting passengers off at a stop just outside the embassy walls with no idea where it was going. Somehow, at that very moment, it didn't matter one bit.

When her heart stopped hammering quite so loudly, Janey dug through her backpack for her guidebook and tried to work out, from the passing street signs, just where they were headed.

The bus wasn't at all crowded, and Janey felt a little shy about standing up and approaching the elderly couple several rows back, or the loud gang of teenage boys lounging just by the doors, and asking them in broken Italian where they were going.

She fanned her face and looked about with more interest. The bus wound its way up and down narrow streets, the driver venting loud volleys of frustrated Italian as mopeds, motorbikes and pedestrians charged in and out of his path. The entire city seemed to live life in fast-forward and Janey was fascinated to see Rome's citizens co-existing with so much ancient history. Turn a corner, and beside a fenced-off pile of broken marble columns there might be a tiny grocery store or wine bar plying its trade, above which would be apartments crammed with ordinary families going about their business, toddlers playing on the narrow balconies overhead while their mothers hung out washing, or in one case, splashing about in an old tin bath while the bus passed several metres below.

As she sat back and watched parts of Rome she'd never seen before rattle by, and life go on at its peculiarly Roman pace, she began to relax. Fellini didn't seem real any longer. It felt like he was worlds away and she chided herself for losing her nerve.

If Luca *wasn't* Fellini, she wouldn't blame him if he thought she'd suddenly developed bipolar disorder where he was concerned. But if he *was*, and Janey shuddered at the thought, then a big fat cold shoulder was what he deserved, and more!

The bus turned onto a major thoroughfare jam-packed with bleating traffic. Janey stood and craned her neck out the half-open window above her head, desperate to find a street sign anywhere, and was rewarded when the bus screeched to a stop just beside a sign that read, rather grandly, 'Corso Vittorio Emanuele II'.

Janey hastily located the right street map and worked out that she was near the bottom end of the Piazza Navona, an oval-shaped public 'square' that she'd visited with Luca, that magical afternoon when he'd just seemed like a gorgeous guy with no agenda. In the past, the Piazza Navona had been a vast stadium where ancient Romans had raced chariots or something, but now it was filled with the roar of three iconic fountains and the chatter of hundreds of tourists guzzling gelati and iced drinks, taking photos of the same things.

She remembered that they'd run out of time to explore the fascinating street of antique dealers that ran off the northern end of the piazza, the Via dei Coronari. 'That is for a whole other day,' Luca had said laughingly, when Janey had expressed a desire to browse the antique shops for a souvenir to take home. 'There are so many, and some so specialised, that you would need days to view the wares, and then more, to haggle with the dealers. Some have been there for centuries, in one guise or another.'

Janey jumped off outside the baroque façade of a public museum, and made for a nearby laneway that led right up to the southern end of the Piazza Navona.

Glad to be out of the crowded bus in the slightly less stuffy heat of the afternoon, she grabbed a granita from one of the cafés facing the piazza before wending her way through the posing tourists and souvenir vendors in the square. She made a beeline for the street of antiques.

Luca had been right. The street was one peeling façade after another, housing more antiques than she'd ever seen in her life. She browsed a store that sold old prints, some from as early as the sixteenth century and extremely rare and fragile. She purchased a tiny, framed etching of some Italian wildflowers from the eighteenth century for Gabs's parents – to thank them for helping her get back on her feet – and strolled on, peering in the windows of a dealer who sold Roman and Etruscan era marble busts, and another who sold only gilded, religious icons. She stopped to wander through a long, cool showroom of modernist Italian advertising memorabilia and twentieth-century furniture, smiling at the woman fanning herself with an art catalogue at the cashier's desk, before heading into the tiny shop front of a dealer who sold Italian paintings from the nineteenth and twentieth centuries.

'Buongiorno, signorina,' smiled the handsome young art dealer. He was seated in a faded deck chair at the back of the store, in front of a retro 1950s electric fan that was on at full blast. A plate with the remains of a sandwich on it sat at his feet. He returned to reading an Italian paperback, allowing Janey to browse at her leisure.

She stole a sideways glance at him. He looked like he was in his late twenties, and had a mop of dark curling hair and the sensitive features and dark soulful eyes of a poet or intellectual. Libby had been so right about Italian guys! Janey smiled, flicking slowly through rack after rack of oil paintings displaying Italian street and beach scenes, the canals of Venice, ancient ruins, and portraits of long-dead people. Some were so realistic, it was as though her eyes were connecting with them through an open window of time.

After making her way around the shop, she was drawn back to a tiny oil painting of a towering arched ironwork gate, framing what looked like a square containing an Egyptian obelisk on one side and a grand, domed church on the other. She couldn't work out where this place was, but the glimpse of the square beyond the open gate was archetypal Rome. For upon the cobbled square could be glimpsed a tiny taxi, some passing cars, and a distant scattering of people strolling in the sunshine.

'Quanto?' she asked, holding up the painting to the angelic looking young man in the deckchair, unsure whether he spoke English. 'E dove?' she added, feeling tongue-tied. She wanted to find out where this magical place could possibly be, but her Italian was so bad she'd probably just asked after the health of his cat!

The young man laid down his book and wandered over to take a look at the painting she held in her hand, with its peeling backing paper and tacky frame. Janey crossed her fingers that it wouldn't cost more than she had with her, because she'd never wanted to own a painting more than she wanted this one.

He turned it over in his hands several times.

The young man finally replied in accented English, 'Good choice, Miss. This is a pleasant view of Santa Maria di Montesanto and the obelisco at the Piazza del Popolo from beneath the arch of the Porta del Popolo. It is late twentieth century,' he explained, pointing out the taxi and cars. 'So it is not so much. For you, I make 150 euro. It is well worth such price. It is very fine.'

Janey tried to hide her disappointment, working out that the little painting was over two hundred dollars – her entire budget for several days in Rome! She took the painting back from the man, regretfully tucking it back where she'd found it.

'Mi dispiace.' She shook her head. 'I can't afford it. But it's been lovely meeting you.'

She turned to step back out of the shop when the young man called, 'Wait! I am mistaken.'

He rummaged through the pile of paintings Janey had just left and drew out the tiny oil again. 'Fifty euro, okay? The frame, it is not so good. And see, the back, eh?' He picked at the peeling paper with a fingernail. 'It will need the changing.'

Janey smiled broadly at the young man's gallantry, because clearly the painting was worth more than fifty euros, regardless of the frame's condition. He hadn't made a mistake, she knew, he was being kind, and Janey's heart soared because she could afford fifty euros *and* she could have her little slice of Rome forever!

'Deal,' she said, then frowned. 'If you're sure?'

The young man nodded, and wrapped the little painting securely in brown paper and string before handing it to her. She emptied her wallet gladly, and they smiled at each other as the young man accepted her scrounged-together pile of notes and coins.

'You will come again before you leave Rome?' said the young man, more as a command than a question. 'I am Gabriel Sansovino.' He held out a hand to be shaken.

'And I'm Janey Gordon,' she beamed. 'And I will most certainly return. You have a lovely shop.'

Gabriel Sansovino inclined his head and replied cheerfully, 'Alla prossima volta! Ciao, till next time,' before returning to his deckchair, sandwich, book and fan.

Brandon

Celia and Janey reached home at almost the same time.

'Is everything all right?' Celia asked when she spotted Janey in her bedroom placing the small, wrapped oil painting carefully into her suitcase. 'Libby said you weren't feeling well – apparently you bolted out of the Ambassador's rooms as if you'd seen a ghost! She started telling me some garbled story about you, but the Ambassador interrupted us before I could make sense of what she was saying. Is there anything you need to tell me?' Her expression was faintly disapproving.

Janey flushed, knowing her behaviour around Celia had been perceived as pretty flaky to date! Unsure whether Libby had updated Celia on her problems with Fellini, Janey said, 'Sorry I ran out on you, but I *was* feeling really bad . . .' Her voice trailed off. She wanted to tell Celia what had been happening, but equally she didn't want Celia to think even less of her. Her story *was* rather strange. Where did she start? 'Um . . .'

Celia didn't give her a chance to clarify things, interrupting gently, 'Well, as long as you've combatted whatever nasty bug that was – though I must say you seem to have recovered very quickly – we can reschedule the embassy tour. It isn't going anywhere. But I've got another treat in store for you for tomorrow morning that we *will* have to act on quickly, because tickets to the Raffaello exhibition are hot property at the moment and all entries are timed. You're going to *love* it!'

She beamed at Janey, who tried hard not to look blank. Obviously, Libby hadn't managed to tell Celia about Fellini and Janey was loath to bring the subject up with Celia so excited for her about the exhibition. *Raffaello?* She thought wildly. Wasn't that a type of, uh, chocolate?

Celia smiled, as though Janey had spoken aloud. 'One of the leading artists of the Italian High Renaissance. Otherwise known to the English-speaking world as *Raphael*. You might have seen his tomb in the Pantheon. A couple of our staff members didn't take up their tickets, so you and Freddy – lucky things! – get to go. Freddy will be home later tonight – she's having dinner with her father.' As Celia backed out of the room, she told Janey to dress casually for dinner at a local osteria just around the corner from the apartment.

After her aunt had gone, Janey's expression grew thoughtful. Maybe there would be a chance to bring the subject of Fellini up with Celia later. As she changed for dinner, she made an amused face at her own reflection. Somehow, Freddy didn't strike her as much of an art lover! It would be an interesting morning, no doubt.

Celia saw them both down to the car the next day. Janey had only just learnt that Luca was driving them to the exhibition at the Museo Galleria e Borghese – the sixteenth-century art gallery that had originally been the palace of the aristocratic Borghese family, located within the lovely gardens where she'd shared a picnic lunch with Luca on her very first day in Rome – and she had to concentrate hard on keeping her expression neutral, what with Celia watching her every move!

'Buongiorno, signorina Gordon e signorina Del Gigli,' murmured Luca formally as first Janey, then Freddy, climbed into the back seat.

'Have fun, girls!' Celia sighed. 'I wish I was going with you, instead of to that boring seminar on Eastern Bloc policies.'

Janey waved out the window to her aunt, stung by the thought that she still hadn't managed to update Celia on what had been going on. Her aunt had been so upbeat and chatty at dinner the night before that Janey hadn't dared to bring up the subject for fear of causing any more tension.

Freddy sank down low in her seat and maintained a sullen silence. She started needling Luca in Italian as soon as he left the kerb, excluding Janey from the conversation. But Luca would have none of it.

'Speak English,' he said. 'Janey, she cannot understand us. It is rude.'

'Well, she's welcome to listen,' Freddy shrugged, 'but it's got nothing to do with her anyway! Sorry Janey, but this is between me and extreme-failure-to-commit over here. Why won't you say *yes*, amico mio?'

Janey tried very hard not to look as if she was eavesdropping and stared out her window as if she couldn't care less about the intriguing conversation swirling around her.

'Because you are not yet sixteen!' said Luca testily, as if they'd had this discussion many times before. 'Your mother, she is my boss! She will not like that I take you out dancing.'

'I've got fake ID,' Freddy wheedled. 'And you know when I'm totally made up and dressed to kill I can pass for a uni student.'

The pair broke back into impatient Italian and their heated exchange continued until Freddy finally snarled in English, 'Fine. *Fine*! Have it your way, *caro*. You're missing out! Now this whole trumped-up expedition is a waste of my time. Mother knows I *hate* art, so you'll forgive me, Janey,' she shot Janey a sharp glance, 'if I ask Luca to drop me at Luz's on the way to the Galleria Borghese. And don't bother telling my mother about this little unscheduled detour of mine, Luca, or I'll make more trouble for you than you can even envisage.'

'You 'ave already made plenty for me!' Luca replied tersely.

'Well, it's easy enough to fix,' Freddy spat. 'Just say *yes*.'

Luca remained silent, his profile tight-lipped.

'Um,' Janey piped up from her corner.

'Um nothing.' Freddy said. 'I'm on *holiday*. And holidays

and creepy old renaissance paintings are mutually exclusive in my book.'

Janey didn't bother to point out that she was on holiday too and that creepy old renaissance paintings weren't really her thing either.

'Anyway, seen one Raffaello, seen 'em all. Take me to Luz's place, Luca. *Now*.' Freddy's tone bordered on petulant.

'Okay,' said Luca. 'It is as you wish.' They had almost reached the Gallery by way of the Viale delle Belle Arti, but Luca did as Freddy ordered and turned the car around, heading in the direction of the exclusive residential area of Parioli, where Luz's very wealthy family owned a seventeenth-century palazzo.

After Freddy flounced out of the car without another word, slamming the door in a fit of pique before being admitted into the imposing grey stone palazzo by a grave-looking manservant, Janey and Luca were alone in the car together. It had all happened so quickly that Janey only just remembered that she should, by rights, be very nervous about that development!

'She is hard work, that one,' said Luca. 'You will enjoy the exhibition a little more, I think? Now she 'as gone.'

Janey smiled, though her intrigue remained at the depth of feeling Freddy seemed to harbour for Luca. He really *was* a heartbreaker. 'I feel more relaxed already,' she murmured.

Luca gave her a fleeting grin over his shoulder as he did what felt like the umpteenth u-turn that day.

They lapsed into silence as Luca took several shortcuts

near the splendid Villa Glori park and headed in the direction of the Galleria Borghese once more.

'May I ask,' said Luca after a while, 'whether your bad humour with me – it has improved?'

Janey couldn't help but smile again at the elaborate politeness of Luca's pointed question. She decided to do some conversational digging around of her own. Two could play at this game!

Keep your friends close, and your enemies closer, she thought.

'Sorry if it seemed that way to you,' she said neutrally, 'but I've had a few things on my mind. One of them being that some juvenile prankster has got hold of my Italian mobile number and is sending me repulsive text messages.'

Luca shot her a startled look in the driver's mirror.

Janey pulled out her mobile phone with a show of great reluctance and read the most recent message to him, all the while watching his eyes in the mirror.

'When did you receive this?' he snapped. 'Yesterday? At the embassy?'

It was amazing how quick he was, she thought. *If he didn't send it!*

'Yes,' she said simply.

'Well, that explains many things!' he replied with the air of a man who had just solved a particularly difficult puzzle. 'The number? What is it?'

Janey recited the mystery caller's number and Luca surprised her by saying, 'Let us dial it. *Now*. We shall see who this – this joker is.' And he punched the number into his mobile phone, which was plugged into the car's hands-free system. In a second, the sound of the mystery mobile's dial tone came over the car's speakers.

Janey shivered. Maybe Fellini would actually pick up! She leant forward intently as the connection was established.

'Pronto?' someone answered, in a deep voice. Janey breathed in raggedly. The caller had just confirmed her suspicions – Fellini *was* a man!

Luca only had time to snap, 'Chi parla? Mi chiamo Luca Sarti...' before whoever it was hung up, without saying another word.

'Sprung!' said Janey excitedly. 'That sounded like a pretty guilty response to me. Is there any way we can trace that number and find out who he *really* is?'

'Not unless you make the complaint,' Luca responded as he eased the car into a parking spot a short walking distance from the main entrance of the Villa Borghese. He turned and looked at her searchingly. 'You wish to do that? There are many – how do you say – *formalities*, but it is possible. I can help.'

He seemed so sincere that Janey's doubts about him melted away. How could she have thought he was the one behind Fellini's antics when he'd actually *dialled the guy's number* and been prepared to stand up to him? Her heart skipped a beat. She wouldn't have had the guts to do the same thing, it hadn't even occurred to her to take the fight right up to Fellini that way.

'If he tries it again, I might take you up on that,' she said.

'Deal,' Luca replied, adding, 'but you must tell me if this man, he troubles you again? And if you find you are free this Saturday afternoon, my sister Lucia and her friends, they meet at the Stazione Termini at noon to take the train once more to Ostia. And she would still love to 'ave your company, as would I.'

Charmed, Janey's heart flipped over again, and she wondered what all the girlfriends could possibly be doing that Luca had time to go to the beach with *her*.

Somehow, despite everything that had happened so far, she found herself saying bemusedly that *yes, a beach trip sounds rather lovely* as she slid out of the back seat, waving as Luca drove away.

Privately, Janey had been dreading the art exhibition, probably as much as Freddy. She didn't mind wandering through a decorated church, but she didn't think an actual exhibition of heavy religious pictures was her bag. Some saint was usually involved, for one thing, dying in a horribly complicated way. She loved her new painting of Rome – that kind of stuff she could relate to – but an exhibition of paintings by some prodigy of the Italian High Renaissance sounded about as exciting as a cold bath.

But as Janey absorbed the high-ceilinged rooms of the Villa Borghese – filled with marble, gold leaf, cherubs, saints, busts and countless other fanciful things, among which Raffaello's artworks were lovingly placed – she was pleasantly surprised.

Sure, it had to be said that there was *a lot* of death and dying in the Raffaello exhibition, but the portraits were astonishing. There was an intimate painting of a dark-eyed woman in an elaborate peach silk dress and long simple veil dated 1514–15 – how long ago! – that seemed to glow with an inner life and light. Janey was just turning away from the haunting portrait of a grave-eyed, flaxen-haired young woman with a unicorn when Brandon appeared beside her.

As usual, he looked good enough to be on the cover of an international men's fashion mag. But seeing him here, when she hadn't expected to run into anyone she knew, caused Janey's insides to go icy.

'What are *you* doing here?' she gasped. She recalled Em's words about the bizarre coincidence strike rate where she and Brandon were concerned and waited tensely to hear him out.

'I've decided to take you out to a late lunch,' he offered with a grin. 'I was at Luz's place when Freddy blew in like a tornado and said she felt bad about standing you up because she *hates* art. While I, on the other hand, *love* Renaissance painting, and you can't get much better than our old friend Raffaello here – absolute prodigy, dead at thirty-seven from too much hard living – so I begged her to give me her ticket and came in search of you. Two birds with one stone. How perfect.'

Brandon's charming confession had an instantly calming effect on Janey, who wondered dazedly whether it might be possible that Brandon truly had a thing for her. The thought was astonishing, but heart-warming, all at the same time.

'Have you seen everything?' Brandon continued, tucking one of Janey's hands through the crook of his elbow as he steered her through the slow-moving crowd of tourists. She nodded happily, 'My favourite has to be *La donna velata*.'

Brandon grinned. '*Woman with a veil*,' one of Raffaello's supreme achievements. It *is* rather astonishing. It's on loan from the Palazzo Pitti in Florence.'

'It seems to, I don't know, *glow*. Like the surface is, um, illuminated. But what would I know? I'm no art critic.' Janey hoped she didn't sound lame.

'I like his more bloodthirsty creations myself,' Brandon responded confidently. 'Which is why we're blowing this joint now. Too many portraits. Let's grab something at the Hotel Hassler's rooftop restaurant – the Imàgo.' Janey wondered if those places should mean anything to her.

'My father practically runs his business from there, the food's so superb! And don't get me started on the view. It's only a short walk. If it's good enough for TomKat, well, it's good enough for us, huh? We deserve it after our morning of artistic edification.'

Janey's brow cleared and she accepted happily, hoping that she had enough in her wallet to get past ordering an entrée. They strolled through an area of the Villa Borghese gardens that Janey hadn't been through before, chancing almost magically upon the Hotel Hassler, situated at one of the park's edges. It was an amber-coloured building at the top of the Spanish Steps near the Trinità dei Monti church. As the liveried doorman swung wide the glass entry doors and they entered the marbled and mirrored reception area, Brandon finished listing the unbelievable roster of celebrities who'd stayed or dined there. 'Audrey Hepburn, Princess Diana, the Kennedys, Suri Cruise...' as Janey listened with starry eyes. 'And now *you*,' he added suavely.

'And now *me*,' Janey replied, a little breathless from the walk, the heat, and maybe the company. Brandon was beginning to grow on her, she thought. *Just a little.* He was a bit *too* confident and a shocking name-dropper, but if you looked like he did and were stinking rich to boot, there was probably good reason!

'It only gets better,' said Brandon, as they entered the restaurant and looked out on the panorama of Rome's rooftops and spires. Janey thought it had to be one of the most romantic restaurants she had ever seen. The view – not to mention the ambience of acres of dark wood, velvet, crystal and Venetian glass – was staggering.

She looked down on the Piazza di Spagna as the discreet waiter in white tie led them to a table next to one of the towering windows. 'It looks so different from up here,' she said dreamily, recalling how Brandon had found her, near tears, in that very square the other day.

They enjoyed a lunch of tagliatelle with truffle sauce, and as they ate, Janey and Brandon found themselves in violent agreement – from books they'd read and movies they'd seen, to places they wanted to visit one day.

'Definitely Patagonia,' said Janey after they'd both agreed that India and Bhutan were definitely in their top five, and

Brandon had finished describing his recent trek with six close friends to the Inca city of Machu Picchu.

'Bruce Chatwin,' Brandon replied with instant recognition. '*In Patagonia* made me want to drop everything and go there too! I *so* agree. Slap that into the top five as well.'

If he isn't perfect, he's damn well close, Janey thought with a smile as Brandon toasted her with a glass of lemon, lime and bitters and summoned the waiter for the dessert menu.

Janey excused herself after they ordered their coffees. 'I won't be long,' she said as their waiter discreetly indicated the direction of the restaurant's bathroom.

'It will still feel like an eternity,' Brandon grinned rakishly. 'Hurry back now!'

As she returned to the table, Janey's step slowed as she caught the sound of Brandon's mobile ringtone. Of course, it had to be the ultra-slick 'What Goes Around . . . Comes Around' by Justin Timberlake! Brandon was an all-round classy guy, Janey smiled to herself.

But as she got closer to the back of his seat, he sounded like he was in the middle of a heated argument with another . . . girl!

'Look, bella mia,' he hissed, not realising Janey was standing just behind him, 'it's kind of tricky at the moment. I'm in the middle of something. No can do, babe.'

Janey sucked in a deep breath as she hovered behind Brandon's chair. Did he have a *girlfriend*? she wondered, suddenly stricken. She was pretty new to all this stuff and didn't know if having unseen competition was well . . . normal with a guy like Brandon.

'You know you're always my first priority,' Brandon added softly into the phone. 'You're my number one, remember?'

Janey flushed. She waited until he snapped his phone shut before striding noisily up to the table, so that he turned.

'Who was that?' Janey asked brightly, as if she hadn't been listening in on him for the last couple of minutes.

Brandon shrugged distantly, 'My mom.'

'Look,' he added, clearly uncomfortable, 'do you mind if we cancel the coffees? I've suddenly remembered something I had to do. We'll do this again, yeah? It's been a blast.'

Janey nodded unhappily as Brandon signalled for the bill, paying for the coffees they'd never received and the desserts they hadn't had a chance to finish, because cost meant nothing to somebody like him.

They were silent as they rode the lift down together. It was as though the Brandon she'd only just been joking and laughing with had been replaced by a pale imitation. Something was definitely bothering him.

'Have fun shopping!' he muttered distractedly after Janey murmured that she might hit the stores on the nearby Via del Corso and pick up some Alessi gadgets for her friends, having noticed how inexpensive they were in Rome. She'd been hoping he would join her, but after they left the hotel he turned and strode back in the direction of the Borghese Gardens.

Janey drifted down the Spanish Steps towards the Piazza di Spagna, wondering what had just happened.

She was surprised to feel so shattered, because she hadn't expected to get hooked on Brandon's company so quickly. She had thought that he was genuinely interested in her, but suddenly she wasn't so sure. Especially if he was running some kind of harem behind her back!

Loaded with quirky giftware for her closest mates, Janey returned to the apartment in the early evening. Surprisingly, Freddy was home, flicking through some back issues of Italian *Vogue* in the apartment's living room.

'Hey,' said Freddy in a friendly tone, looking up as Janey trailed past with her shopping bags.

'Hey yourself,' Janey replied, but she kept walking, too puzzled about Brandon's weird behaviour to want to talk about it with Freddy, should she ask whether he'd caught up with her at the exhibition.

Celia called out gaily from the kitchen, 'Guess who managed to finish up early tonight just to rustle up dinner for my girls? Perfect timing, Janey! You've got that trip to Pompeii tomorrow, right?' Janey nodded, hovering in the doorway. 'So I thought I'd make sure you ate a big dinner and got enough rest. It's meant to be forty-five degrees in the shade tomorrow, Pompeii is *huge*, plus you've got an early start.'

Janey smiled at her aunt, placing her shopping bags in her bedroom before swinging onto a bar stool in the kitchen.

'Been shopping?' Celia asked as she slid portions of herb-crusted sea bass onto beds of homemade ratatouille. She pushed a plate towards Janey and called out to Freddy to come and eat. Freddy slouched into the kitchen and slid onto the stool beside Janey's, poking at her dinner.

'You know I *hate* fish,' she said, pulling a face.

'You hate lots of stuff,' said Celia. 'Eat up. Your brain could use it. So how was the Raffaello exhibition?'

'*Bor*-ing,' Freddy replied, 'like I thought it would be.' She shot a pleading sidelong glance at Janey, who looked down at her plate to hide her confusion. Freddy hadn't been there. She was covering her tracks!

Celia frowned. 'That's it?' she said. 'In two syllables? Well, what did *you* think, Janey?'

'The portraits were incredible.' Janey added mischievously, 'Didn't you think so, Freddy?'

Freddy darted another look at Janey. 'I've seen better,' she mumbled, pushing fish around her plate.

'Oh, I doubt it!' said Celia. 'He's acknowledged as one of the best portraitists the human race has ever produced. I wrote my honours thesis on Raffaello.'

'Whatever,' Freddy muttered. Janey looked down as Celia and Freddy glared at each other.

'Well, what else did you two get up to?' Celia asked, popping a forkful of fish into her mouth.

Janey and Freddy raised their eyebrows at each other.

'We pretty much split up as soon as we got there,' said Freddy.

'We sure did,' Janey agreed. 'In fact, Freddy's friend Brandon met me there and we ended up having lunch together at the

Hotel Hassler.'

This time Celia's eyebrows shot up. 'The Hotel Hassler?' she cried. 'At the newly revamped Imàgo restaurant?'

Janey nodded. 'It was pretty spectacular.'

'You mean,' Celia said, putting her fork down, 'that you left Freddy at the exhibition while you went off with one of *her* friends to have lunch at the Hassler? Only one of the most expensive five-star hotels in the city? Why didn't you ask her to go too?'

Freddy grinned mischievously this time. 'Yeah, why *didn't* you ask me? I could have hung out with you two, instead of catching the rest of the exhibition all on my own. I would have loved to have a stickybeak at the Hassler!'

Janey bit her lip. Correcting Celia's false impression that Freddy had attended the Raffaello exhibition would make the two of them look bad. Freddy for lying in the first place, and Janey for covering it up! It was a no-win situation. 'Um, I don't know,' she mumbled, deciding the more honourable thing to do was back Freddy up. 'Sorry, didn't think.'

'No you didn't,' Celia said in a low voice. 'I must say that I'd thought better of you, Jane. You're older than Federica, and you should be looking out for her, instead of dumping her somewhere and making off with one of her best friends.'

'Who also just happens to be supremely good looking and *very* loaded,' Freddy chipped in.

Celia started washing dishes furiously as the girls got up to leave the table. 'I don't think I've ever encountered someone quite as boy crazy as you are, Janey Gordon. It's Luca one day, Brandon the next. I can't keep up with you! I'm not sure what kind of role model you'd be for my daughter . . .'

Freddy quickly hauled Janey out of the kitchen before she could open her mouth to defend herself.

Pompeii

'Thanks,' Freddy laughed as she yanked Janey up the hallway towards her bedroom. 'I owe you one!'

Janey made an outraged gargling sound and Freddy giggled.

'Mum doesn't like me hanging out at Luz's place because she thinks Luz is a spoilt, snobby diva with an attitude problem. And she's right! But it's still fun to see how the other half lives! Luz has got what her family grandly calls "retainers" but I'd call personal *slaves*. She's waited on hand and foot. *Nothing's* too much trouble. Scrambled eggs and Sevruga caviar at three in the morning? No problem! Her dad's some kind of duke or something, and her mum's a Colombian coffee baron's daughter. They are *off-the-scale* rich.' She pushed Janey inside her room and shut the door.

'Because I just protected your backside *again*,' Janey

spluttered, 'y-your mum thinks I'm some kind of a . . .' She'd just about had it up to there with saving Freddy from Celia's wrath when all Freddy seemed to do was dump her in it!

Freddy shrugged nonchalantly. 'You'll be gone soon, and she'll forget about it. Don't take things so seriously! You wanna hang out tonight? My buds and I are hitting the Duke's bar in Parioli, then moving on to the Jackie O for some dancing. Brandon will be there,' Freddy added cheekily. 'We don't have any fake ID for you, but I can make you up to look way older than you actually are. So it should be a cinch to get in.'

Remembering Brandon's suspicious phone call at lunch, Janey replied stiffly, 'Thanks, but no thanks, I think I'll pass.' She didn't think she could stand losing Freddy and her friends in the crowd again, especially at some venue she'd never been to before, filled with potential sleaze buckets! And if Brandon looked right through her again, like he had today, she wasn't sure how she'd handle it.

'Suit yourself.' Freddy started buzzing around her bedroom, blinging up for her big night. Still seething, Janey let herself out and hit the shower.

Later that night, still a little upset by how her day had turned out, Janey headed down the silent hallway to the study and logged into her MySpace page. While her last posting had been all about Luca, her latest one was all about Brandon and how he'd basically blown her off at the end of their swanky date. She needed help working through it all.

What do U think? Reckon he's got a girlfriend stashed away somewhere? Thoughts + input please. Real confused.

It was late enough her time that Em and Gabs had just woken up back home and were online at their respective computers. Janey refreshed her page a few times with a smile on her face and was soon rewarded with Em's first comment.

Hey babe. Still think u shld give Luca benefit of doubt. Brandon sounds GROSS blowin hot / cold dat way. *The Divine Miss Em*

Gabs, who was busy catching up with a bunch of other people, took a little longer to chime in.

O, I concur. Brandon = rich brat playing w U ♥. Luca = happily eva after. *Gabstar*

Not sure what to think. Brandon beautiful one moment, freezing the next! *x X Janey G X x*

The three of them messaged back and forth for another half hour until Em wrote:

Catch u tonight ur time maybe? Signed up for 1 day script writing master class. Big name

American out to tell it like it is in HOLLYWOOD! Gotta motor. Easy.

The Divine Miss Em

Pretty soon after, Gabs signed off too.

Im out!

Gabstar

Janey updated her page with a few holiday snaps, including one of Brandon and a sneaky profile shot of Luca she'd taken one morning as he was driving Celia away to her office. He looked like a secret agent of some kind, in shades, with tousled hair. She also added a comment about how much she was looking forward to her trip to Pompeii the next day, promising to upload more photos on her return. She refreshed her page one more time and was on the verge of logging out herself when she noticed a new comment had been posted.

Fellini was back, poisonous as ever.

Like a person who looks like u could ever pull guys like dat!   *Fellini*

There was a tiny orange and green 'Online Now' icon under his avatar. Janey was so angry she was shaking. Who *was* this freak? How dare he get so personal and in her face? Especially *here*. It was supposed to be *My*Space, not OpinionatedKookSpace. She felt violated.

Get off my page! JERK. No one asked U.

x X Janey G X x

Janey waited to see how Fellini would reply, adrenaline roaring through her body. It was frightening, but also kind of empowering, dealing with this cretin head on. Fellini shot back seconds later.

 JERK best u can do? u need ME to keep uself REAL. U getting ideas, chicken head. *Fellini*

Fellini was feeling talkative this evening, Janey thought distastefully as she typed back.

 Who asked u? u and me r nothing.
LEAVE ME ALONE. x X Janey G X x

 That's right. u and me r nothing, and it stays that way! And LEAVE is the operative word. U leave, it stops. And not B4. Get it? *Fellini*

Janey hurriedly logged off, feeling like she'd been slimed. If she'd only gone with Freddy and her friends to Duke's Bar, she would've avoided this little confrontation! Although the way she'd left things with Brandon, a night at Duke's might only have been marginally better, she told herself grimly.

Suddenly she was glad to be leaving in just over a week. The trip of a lifetime had suddenly become a nightmarish game with rules she hadn't a hope of understanding. She couldn't wait to go home to her non-judgemental friends and her low-key life. Thanks to Fellini, Rome had suddenly turned from a magical place into a frightening one.

Janey suddenly missed her mum so much it was like a physical pain and hot tears spilled down her cheeks.

Janey woke the next morning to a sky as dull and overcast as her mood. She slipped into her freshly laundered orange tank and white shorts, because the forecast for where she was headed was sizzling. Celia had already gone to the office and Freddy had no doubt crashed at Luz's or somewhere, because the apartment was all Janey's as usual.

She resisted the urge to log on again to find out whether Fellini had caused new mischief on her page overnight, deciding instead to head out for a strong coffee and a little breakfast before boarding the bus that would take her down to the archaeological ruins of Pompeii. Ever since she'd learnt in history class about the city that had been lost for almost two thousand years after Mount Vesuvius had erupted and buried it in layers of ash and rubble, she'd wanted to see it. So when she'd been invited to go to Rome, it had been pretty easy for Janey to jump on the web and work out that Pompeii was only three and a half hours away. She'd organised a day tour from the comfort of Gabs's place and now all she had to do was show up at Rome's Termini Station and board a bus. The same place Luca had suggested she meet him, his sister and their friends for a trip to Ostia in a couple of days' time.

Just thinking about Luca, and about Brandon, made her head hurt. She didn't know what to believe about either of them, and was determined to put them out of her mind for the day and just enjoy the tour. The bus was scheduled to head south from Rome along the delightfully named Highway of the Sun, with a stop in Naples for lunch, then a two-hour tour of Pompeii.

Janey worked out that she'd get back to Rome by about eight that evening. Plenty of time for Fellini to wreak more havoc on her MySpace page, she thought, as she stopped at an espresso bar near Termini station and ordered a macchiato and a sweet Italian doughnut, or zeppola, to go with it.

Soon after, she boarded the tour bus with a nice Spanish couple, three elderly Canadians, a New Zealand guy, and a Hungarian couple with a toddler son. Taking her seat, she suddenly broke into a sunny smile; Fellini could text his heart out today, but unless he'd booked a ten-hour tour to Pompeii at exactly the same time as she had, he'd have to cool his toxic little backside back in Rome without her!

Janey reclined back in her seat and pulled out an apple. 'Here's to a Fellini-free day!' she told herself as the bus pulled away from the terminal with a roar. Janey bit into the apple with relish and looked out the window with sparkling eyes.

It was after nine in the evening by the time they re-entered the outskirts of Rome, and all Janey wanted was a cool shower and to upload photos to her MySpace to share with her friends.

First, she'd strolled the seaside boardwalks surrounding the serenely blue Bay of Naples, then eaten a huge three-course lunch at a hillside taverna overlooking the modern town of Pompeii. A guide had taken her tour group through the high points of the first-century ruins of ancient Pompeii before leaving each of them to wander the eerily well-preserved city under blazing blue skies.

Here and there among the ruined homes, shops, public baths, temples, amphitheatres, public squares and villas, Janey had chanced upon the scarily lifelike plaster casts of Pompeii's people, lying exactly as they'd fallen. Some parts of the city were still so intact – the cobbled streets and laneways in such perfect condition – that she almost expected to see the ancient Pompeiani emerge from shadowy doorways and go about their business. She wished her friends could have seen the place for themselves. Astonishingly, parts of the original multicoloured frescos and mosaics that had adorned the walls of Pompeii's homes and public buildings were still visible. It was hard to believe that it was a ghost town, and had been for centuries.

The only hitch to an otherwise ideal day was when the tour bus broke down with a transmission problem just outside a rest stop in the middle of nowhere. As tour bus after tour bus had rolled past, disgorging its hot and tired passengers, then rolled out again after everyone had had their obligatory toilet stop and overpriced snack, Janey and her tour group were still there, waiting for the replacement bus to come and get them.

As the bus finally lumbered back to the drop-off point near the Termini Station, Janey swapped email addresses with the friends of all ages that she'd made on her tour, promising to write. Apart from the delay in getting home, she decided, as she started walking slowly back in the direction of Celia's apartment, the trip had been a real highlight of her holiday so far. She'd felt so incredibly free and anonymous. Her mobile hadn't even rung once.

As if to remind her that it was there, however, it buzzed now and Janey tensed, taking a quick look around her at the small groups of people moving languidly by. It was dinnertime for many Romans, and the sidewalk cafés were packed. Perhaps it was Celia asking her out to dinner.

With her radar fine-tuned for trouble, though, she didn't think so.

Janey stopped, thumbed the mobile warily, and read:

What kept u?

She dropped the phone back inside her bag as though it was made of molten lava and picked up her pace. Immediately, it buzzed again.

Don't look at it! Janey told herself. *It's what* he *wants.*

But halfway up Via Volturno her curiosity got the better of her, and she snatched it up again.

U look like something the cat dragged in. Orange is SO not ur colour.

Janey began to run.

Città Universitaria

Going by memory alone, Janey ducked and wove her way through the warren of streets to the north of Termini Station, which looked a lot seedier at nightfall than she remembered from only that morning. Those stores that weren't open at this hour had steel shutters pulled tight across their windows, many of which were covered in dense graffi ti, and the streets and lanes were crowded with dingy two or three star hotels. Touts stood outside many of the less popular restaurants and cafés she passed, and they reached out and tried to catch Janey by the arm as she raced by, which only made her more jumpy.

Part of her hoped that if she kept on the move, she would somehow lose the spiteful presence that was intent on making her waking hours a nightmare. But her phone buzzed again, demanding her attention:

Look around! If you dare.

Janey took shelter on the front step of a busy, well-lit pharmacy. Scanning the street, at first she saw nothing out of the ordinary. But apprehension made her look harder and she glimpsed, lounging in the shadowy doorway of an apartment block across the street, a tall figure with curly black hair wearing what looked like a golden *mask*.

It was a carnival mask, the sort Venetians wore in the annual Carnevale. It hid the wearer's face from jaw to hairline, and looked grotesque! The eyes were blank ovals, through which the watcher peered at Janey, and the nose and mouth were taut and emotionless lines.

Janey shrieked and retreated into the shop, asking the first customer she stumbled across where she was. The elderly woman shrugged and rattled off several phrases in Italian with a vigorous waving of hands. The next middle-aged woman Janey tried to approach just shook her head and moved away.

'Does anyone speak English?' Janey called out. 'Please, where *am* I?'

Several people looked up curiously, then went back to what they were doing.

Half-angry, half-terrified, Janey launched herself out of the pharmacy and headed back up the road in a northerly direction, not stopping to see if the shadowy watcher was following.

She knew she'd be in a lot of trouble if she didn't beat Fellini back to Celia's place.

Janey wrapped her fist around her house keys, and started

looking for a taxi she could flag down, all the while getting more and more lost.

Janey was running scared. It might have been her imagination playing tricks on her eyes but she seemed to see shadowy figures everywhere she turned. She'd taken refuge in one crowded bar after another as she made her way uptown, but each time she'd emerged after being hit on a thousand times by over-eager young men, some cute, some definitely not so cute, who all wanted to buy her drinks she couldn't even understand the names of, she thought she saw it again. Just the faintest glint of a gold-masked watcher, waiting. Somewhere just out of sight.

It was late. And Janey was sick of hiding. She just wanted to get back to Celia's and barricade herself inside and not leave again until it was time to go home.

Home. A lump formed in her throat. It felt so far away. Celia had been right, Janey thought sadly, this trip *had* been a mistake. You couldn't force someone to like you, even if they were supposed to be your family and you wanted them to like you so much that it hurt.

Janey wanted to believe that she wasn't hopelessly lost. The threat of that masked watcher, lurking, had caused her to change direction a multitude of times and she was probably ages away from Celia's by now. It was a shock when she emerged from the narrow, bar-filled street she'd been cautiously traversing to find herself facing a busy multi-lane road that ran hard up against a stretch of the old city walls.

She hurried towards the nearest pedestrian crossing and started thumbing frenetically through her guidebook, feeling certain no one would try anything in the presence of so many passing cars.

At that moment, instead of buzzing to indicate a text was coming through, her mobile rang.

Janey almost jumped out of her skin. She scanned the area around her, which was deserted of pedestrians, then scrambled through her backpack for her phone.

It was the first time she'd heard her phone actually *ring* all night. She'd spent so much time skulking around in bars that if it'd rung earlier, she wouldn't have had a hope of hearing it.

As she withdrew it now, the name on the screen took her breath away.

Luca (mobile)

She was so jittery that seeing his name, after all that had already happened, just propelled her into panicky motion. She killed his call immediately, without thinking. She saw that he'd tried to call her at least a dozen times because Luca's name filled the missed-calls screen!

Not waiting for the lights to change in her favour, she dashed across the road, dodging oncoming cars as if her only salvation lay on the other side.

Breathing hard, Janey reached the other side of the Viale Pretoriano and scanned her surroundings. Through a gap in the ancient city walls, ahead of her stretched the gloomily lit Viale dell'Università. She was standing at the top end of an upside-down T-intersection, torn about which way to go.

Should she head back along this side of the Viale Pretoriano in a northerly direction in the hope that it somehow connected up with the Via Nomentana – the main road that would take her back towards Celia's? Or should she continue along the Viale dell'Università and try to find someone to help her get her bearings? On this side of the Viale Pretoriano there was barely any footpath to speak of beneath the shadow of the old Roman fortifications that ran alongside it, and the rushing traffic showed no sign of thinning out any time soon.

Janey hesitated for a moment—but her mind was made up for her when she noticed someone approaching down the Viale Pretoriano. Wearing a white porcelain mask that covered the entire face.

She turned on her heel and started walking quickly in the other direction when another figure, wearing a full gilt and white harlequin mask, stepped calmly out of the traffic further down the street and began moving up towards her. It felt unreal. Like she'd walked into a scene from an Italian *Terminator* movie. She was hemmed in on both sides, and her tormentors were moving closer.

Fellini hadn't given up and gone home—he'd brought reinforcements!

In wordless terror, Janey spun back around and sprinted up the tree-lined Viale dell'Università, which was absolutely deserted. Streetlamps were lit every hundred metres or so, but it was still very dark beneath the cover of the trees, and devoid of life. As she ran – her lungs burning, her backpack banging painfully into her spine – Janey registered that the buildings she passed looked official, like low-rise government office blocks. But few windows were lit and the car parks beneath them were largely empty. Between the harsh rattle of her breathing and her own footfalls, she thought she could hear the unhurried footsteps of her two pursuers echoing behind her. In desperation, she sprinted right at a crossroads and looked around for somewhere to hide. But the door of the first building she tried was locked, and she gave a tiny scream and kept running.

It felt like she'd been running forever when she skidded to a halt in some kind of public square, complete with flagpoles displaying the Italian tri-colour. A street sign told her she was standing in the Piazzale Aldo Moro. A number of darkened roads and streets fanned out from the square in different directions, and she was frantically deciding which one to take when more masked figures appeared silently at the boundaries of the square. There were five in all, including the two that had pursued her from the Viale Pretoriano.

Janey thought her heart would explode with fear! They were closing in on her from all sides, and she had nowhere left to run.

The sound of a car door opening somewhere behind her

made her spin around. She focused her shattered gaze on a grey cement block building with blank mirrored windows. A dark car was parked in front of the building and from beneath one of the building's blunt, rectangular arches *Luca appeared*.

For a moment, Janey stopped breathing.

When she remembered to breathe again, she found herself trapped between the masked youths and Luca's tall and familiar form.

What Brandon had told her had all been true!

All of Janey's terror and rage were in her voice as she screamed at Luca. 'How could you *do* this to me?'

Fellini

Luca held Janey's wild-eyed gaze with his own. 'Cara mia!' he called out. 'Run to me!'

Janey flinched. 'Why would I do that?' she spat. 'After all you've put me through? Do you get off on playing s-sick jokes on girls who like you or something?'

'You are wise not to trust him, Jane,' shouted a male voice in heavily accented English behind her.

Janey turned. It was one of the watchers, the one in the gold mask that she'd first spotted near that pharmacy.

'He is the mastermind,' the speaker added. 'He has set you up from the beginning. All of it is due to Luca Sarti.'

In a flash, Luca's face registered such a look of fury and loathing that Janey instinctively took another step back, away from him and towards the masked people grouped behind her.

'Bugiardo!' Luca roared. 'Liar!'

Uncertainty made Janey's step falter.

In a gentler tone, Luca urged Janey, 'Call Brandon, everything will be clear!'

Janey stared at Luca in confusion for a split second, then grabbed her mobile out of her backpack. Before the watchers behind her registered what she was doing, she'd dialled Brandon's number.

Almost immediately, 'What Goes Around ... Comes Around' cut through the still night air.

Janey spun around.

'You idiot!' said someone, as another of Janey's masked tormentors started laughing.

'You cowards,' said Luca in a ringing voice, 'remove your masks. You are undone by one of your own! Adesso. *Immediately*.'

One by one, Janey's pursuers removed their masks, laughing defiantly, and Janey felt her entire world tilt dangerously for one split second.

For there was *Freddy*, twirling her mask on a finger as though the malevolent looking creation of gold and white porcelain was the latest must-have accessory! And the tall figure in the golden mask had been – who else? – that creep Paolo, while the others revealed themselves to be Luz, Minka and ... *Brandon*.

Janey couldn't bring herself to look at Brandon. She couldn't believe Freddy and her friends had been behind the cruel hoax the entire time.

Fellini wasn't one person – 'he' was five!

'*Why*, Freddy?' Janey gasped. 'What have I ever *done* to you? And Brandon?'

Brandon – the only one who wasn't laughing or smirking – stared at his feet.

Freddy snorted. 'How do you know Luca's not behind it all?' She drifted closer to where Janey stood. 'It's *his* word against *ours*. Blood's thicker than water, remember? He's practically a stranger. He could have put us up to this for his own amusement. You know I've had a crush on him for ages. I'd do anything for Luca, wouldn't I, caro?' she added, blowing a kiss in his direction. 'And my friends would do anything for *me*. Can't you take a joke?'

Paolo snickered, while Luz didn't bother to hide her look of snobby disdain.

'Fermati!' Luca snarled. He turned to Janey and urged, 'Do not believe her, bella mia. She is making trouble.'

Paolo gave an ugly laugh, his expression unapologetic. 'It's what Federica does best! Half the reason she's so fun to be with.'

Minka glanced away in embarrassment, while Brandon just looked sick.

Janey's head was spinning trying to make sense of all the arguments and counter arguments trading back and forth around her. Was Luca the ringleader of the whole thing, or Freddy? *Who* did she believe? She didn't know either of them well enough to tell.

'That's enough!' issued a new voice out of the darkness as

a car door opened nearby. Everyone froze as Celia appeared from the shadows.

Two spots of high colour appeared on Freddy's cheekbones as her look of amusement died.

'I can't tell you how sorry I am,' Celia said to Janey, 'that I believed a single word this *spoilt psychopath* of mine ever told me about you! I don't know how to make it up to you, but it starts *tonight*.'

'It doesn't matter,' Janey replied distractedly, still trying to process Freddy's and Brandon's duplicity.

'And you!' Celia barked in her daughter's direction. 'Get in the car, you disgraceful baggage. And the rest of you,' she took in Freddy's friends with a sweeping glare, 'push off *home*. I'm going to get on the phone to your parents as soon as this is over and I'm making sure they ground each of you for at least the rest of the summer break.'

The histrionics began almost as soon as Luca drove out of the Piazzale Aldo Moro with Janey in the front passenger seat and Celia and Freddy in the back.

'Apologise *now*,' Celia bellowed.

Freddy shook her head mutinously and burst into tears.

Luca and Janey exchanged wry glances.

'What's gotten *into* you lately?' Celia continued more gently over her daughter's bowed head. 'I'd expect you to treat *me* like I've got some sort of leprous disease, but not Janey. Why would you treat her like this? You've always wanted a sibling and then Janey shows up – the next best thing in the circumstances – and what do you do? Try and run her out of our lives! *I don't understand you.*'

'I thought you'd be pleased,' Freddy sobbed. 'Then you'd get to keep *all* the money! And it's not like we need another girl in the family when you don't know what to do with the one you've *got*.'

Janey resisted the urge to turn around. It was between Freddy and Celia, she told herself, though her ears were practically on stalks.

'Whatever do you mean, all the money?' asked Celia incredulously.

'The Gordon money!' Freddy hiccupped. 'If you found her but we didn't get along, remember, because you decided she was *of bad character* – like that stupid will said – we'd get to keep it *all* and wouldn't have to share it.'

Celia shook her head. 'You set all this up so that I'd believe Janey was some kind of ditzy tramp?'

Freddy glared tearfully at her mother.

In the front of the car, Janey frowned, while Luca's straight dark brows shot up. Both maintained their silence, listening intently.

'You mean you knew about the details of the Gordon will?' Celia cried. '*How?*'

'You don't password our home computer,' Freddy responded sullenly. 'I read all the letters you exchanged with the lawyers for the Gordons' estate. Every single one. I've known about that stupid will for ages. *If* you located Lydia Gordon or her child *and* decided that they weren't of bad character, the lawyers would be obliged to distribute half the money to *them*.'

'And you decided to prove Janey's character was of the very worst kind!' Celia sounded flabbergasted. 'I've never wanted all the money, Freddy! I'd much rather have Janey in our lives than keep it all. It's rightfully hers anyway. She *needs* it. We *don't*. I can't believe this was all about the Gordon bequest.'

Janey swallowed through the sudden lump in her throat, remembering how they'd struggled to find the money to pay for her mum's medical expenses. 'The money's pretty useless to me now,' she muttered. 'Freddy can *have* it.'

Freddy ignored her. 'But then we'd be almost as well off as Luz and Brandon are!' she addressed Celia pleadingly. 'And she's a *dork* anyway. She'd never fit in with my crowd. I mean, *look* at her. I gave a her a head-to-toe makeover and she still doesn't know how to dress.'

Freddy really was a piece of work! Janey thought in disbelief. Make-*under*, more like! She was so totally in the wrong, and could still come out with stuff like that!

Luca cleared his throat. 'Brandon did not think so. He took her to the Café de Paris. Perhaps he has not taken *you* there?'

Freddy's eyes were wide with chagrined surprise. 'He didn't tell me about that!' she said, biting her lip angrily. ' And he's been in love with me *forever*. Unreciprocated of course,' she added, darting a quick look at Luca. 'He should've stuck to the script!'

'Enough!' Celia barked. 'We're home now, and we're going

to have it out if it kills us! Every last whinge and gripe and unreasonable demand! It's time you stopped acting like a spoilt princess. I didn't ask for this situation! Your father suddenly decided he wanted to spend the rest of his life with a *doormat* and I wasn't prepared to do that. End of story. Stop pushing it all back on *me*.'

'Fine by me!' said Freddy. 'I don't get enough attention from either of you anyway, without adding another person to the mix! I've got *plenty* to say.' Mother and daughter glared at each other across the back seat.

Luca stopped the car in front of Celia's apartment building and opened the car door for Celia and Freddy before helping Janey out of her seat. Touching her arm, he murmured, 'I may call you?'

Janey, her head still spinning a little from the way things had turned out, nodded shyly. 'You have my number.'

She waved as she entered the building behind her aunt and Freddy. Luca gave a jaunty return blast on the car horn before roaring off at his usual terrifying speed.

It felt to Janey as if she'd last entered the apartment a lifetime ago. So much had happened since that morning.

'How did you find me?' she asked, as Celia shrugged out of her suit jacket in the living room. Freddy attempted to skulk off to her bedroom, but Celia barked, 'You! *Stay*.' Freddy crashed onto an ottoman with her back to them, her arms crossed.

'Just after eight, my inbox pinged,' Celia said, weariness

creeping into her voice. 'I've been so flat out putting the finishing touches to an economic paper on a possible Italian–Australian bilateral free trade agreement that I let a lot of things slip. Including keeping tabs on you and Freddy.'

'So what's new?' Freddy snarled. Celia pointedly ignored her daughter's outburst and continued to study Janey.

'Um, okay,' Janey replied, wondering where Celia was going with all this, but still glad they were *really* talking now.

Celia smiled as she slipped her heavy spectacles off her face, looking instantly younger, less official and very tired. 'I do have a point. I'd accumulated sixty-plus emails since I'd last checked and right near the top I found an email from a Ness McAdams entitled "Attention Celia Albright".'

Janey gaped for a second. '*My* friend Ness?'

Celia nodded as she gestured at Janey to sit. 'Though I couldn't place her at first until I opened her email and saw your name leap out at me from paragraph one. Stupidly, I assumed that it couldn't be important, that she was probably just trying to update you with gossip from home. So I printed and closed the email, then promptly forgot all about it for the next hour or so.'

Janey shook her head. That would probably have been around the time Paolo – in his freaky golden mask – had started stalking her.

'Around ten,' Celia continued, 'Libby – the woman you met the other day, who was stuck working late too – poked her head into my office and asked for a quick word. Turns out she'd been trying to speak to me all week – ever since that day you stood up the Ambassador and embarrassed me horribly – but I just haven't made the time to see her. Something more important kept coming up.' She crinkled her nose apologetically. 'She said it was about *you*, and I'm sorry to say that I demanded to know what it was that you'd done *this* time.'

Janey winced. 'Freddy had pretty much assassinated my character in your eyes by then, so I can understand that.' Freddy made a snorting sound, but it was clear that she was listening intently.

'Well, Libby didn't,' said Celia. 'She'd figured you for who you really were and said it wasn't what *you'd* done, but what someone was doing *to* you. Of course, I had no idea what she was talking about because you hadn't said a word to me! So I ordered her to sit down and spill the beans. She said you'd received a threatening text message while you'd been sitting in the Ambassador's waiting room. You must've been terrified!'

Janey shrugged. 'I was so jumpy by that stage, I wasn't thinking straight! As soon as that text arrived, all I could think of was escaping the embassy, you, Luca, everybody.'

'Your flight reflexes kicked in,' said Celia.

'Bet we gave you a workout,' Freddy muttered.

Janey ignored her. 'I mean, the most sensible thing would've been to sit there and wait for you to get out of your meeting and help me track Fellini down. I mean, it's an Embassy – everyone who goes in and out has to sign. But instead, I just panicked like a dumbbell and *ran*.'

Freddy laughed, making Celia frown.

'*Bolted*, was the word Libby used. She said she was on the phone and saw you drop your mobile with a shriek and hightail it out of there seconds later. *Why* didn't you tell me earlier?' Celia chided Janey. 'Instead of letting me think what Freddy wanted me to think about you?'

Janey smiled. 'Freddy had pretended to be so nice to me – she really had me fooled – and you and I had had a few misunderstandings already . . .'

Celia looked embarrassed.

'. . . so I just decided to stick it out until it was time to head back to Australia. I'm tougher than I look, you know,' Janey added. 'I've kind of had to be.'

'You certainly are,' Celia replied. 'My first impressions of you were so right. You know, sensible, friendly, even a little naïve . . . until my wretched daughter caused me to doubt my own judgment!'

Janey blushed a little at the description.

'Definitely not the crazed man-eater you suddenly seemed to become!' Celia added, shaking her head. 'Every time I saw you, it was Luca this, and Brandon that, and after what I've been through with Freddy chasing Luca all over Rome, having him on speed dial, getting him to drive her and her friends around so much that the Ambassador's had to have a private word with me on more than one occasion . . .' Celia shot her daughter a harassed look.

'You just thought the worst,' said Janey.

'You know what Libby said?' Celia murmured. '"It's Rome – it's practically spelt the same way as *romance*, for heaven's sake!" I tend to forget that, Janey, being the jaded old bird I am. Anyway, as soon as Libby told me what had been happening to you, I went into instant panic mode. Rang home, no one picked up, checked my mobile, no messages, rang your phone, no reply . . .'

'I would've been running for my life just then,' said Janey. 'So I definitely wasn't answering—'

'Right,' Celia agreed, 'so then I rang poor Luca – who was out with his usual crowd of sophisticates . . .'

Freddy turned around at her mother's words, no longer pretending she wasn't interested in the conversation.

'. . . and told him I needed his help,' Celia continued. 'Had this crazy idea that we'd drive around the whole Castro Pretorio district looking for you, because that was the only clue to your whereabouts that I had to go on. I knew you'd gone to Pompeii and I knew what time your tour was supposed to get back—'

'We were seriously delayed,' Janey interrupted wryly.

'. . . and while I was waiting for him, I remembered that mysterious email from Ness McAdams. Turns out it wasn't addressed to *you* after all, it was intended for *me* all along. And it contained your friends' theories about what my sneaky offspring and *her* friends have been up to over the last few days!' It was Celia's turn to glare at Freddy, who just ducked her head.

Celia's expression flickered between disbelief and sheer embarrassment. 'All I knew was that you were about two hours overdue, because you hadn't checked in, and we needed to find you. When Luca pulled up at the Embassy, he said that where you were, Freddy would probably be too, because he had a hunch that Freddy was somehow involved. And he was *right*. Because when you wouldn't take his call either . . .'

'Still running for my life at that point!' said Janey, laughing. It was easy to laugh about it now. 'Plus, there was the possibility he was a crazed loony, so I wouldn't have taken his call either way.'

'He had the presence of mind to call Freddy.' said Celia.

'That rat!' said Freddy angrily. Celia shot her a silencing look.

'He convinced her that he wanted to take her out clubbing at last. And you took the bait!' She looked at Freddy, who looked away. 'Luca has been resisting Freddy's invitations for months. She had no idea I was sitting there listening to the whole conversation, which included several other background voices.'

'Brandon's,' Janey muttered in distress.

Celia nodded. 'We distinctly heard *him* say, "This was a bad idea, Freddy! What are we supposed to do? Just leave her wandering the Città Universitaria on her own, when she's probably hysterical?"'

'Huh! Like he *cared*,' Janey mumbled.

'And Luca and I just stared at each other in shock because it was literally a kilometre away from where *we* were. We knew the Città Universitaria would be as deserted as a graveyard and if you weren't hysterical, it would be a miracle!'

'So what happened next?' said Janey, interested despite herself.

Freddy glared at the ceiling and crossed her arms.

'Though Freddy tried to muffle her mobile, we distinctly overheard her giving the others orders to "close the net" at the Piazzale Aldo Moro and give you one last huge heart attack before calling it a night! Freddy then got back on the line and demanded Luca pick her up at the corner of Viale dell'Università and Viale Pretoriano in twenty minutes, and the rest is history. Now Freddy and I are going to have that little talk because it's way, *way* overdue. I'm really sorry you were drawn into the crossfire, Janey. I never intended your holiday to turn out like this.'

Freddy's expression indicated she was preparing to go on the attack. But before she could open her mouth, Celia said gently, 'I know I've been too wrapped up in work, darling, and you've probably had good reason to act up. You've never let me put my side of the story properly and now you are going to listen. To every word. Really *listen*.'

Janey let herself out of the room as Celia and Freddy began to argue.

As Freddy wailed and Celia talked and paced in the living room, Janey jumped onto her MySpace page to update her friends on the whole mind-bending saga.

'You'll never believe how it all panned out!' she began, in her latest and most anticipated blog ever.

Janey

'You've *got* to be kidding!' Gabs hooted.

Janey was an hour and a half into a hilarious four-way Skype chat with Ness, Em and Gabs – who were all over at Gabs's again – when she heard a tentative knock on the study door. It was about three in the morning Rome time, which equated to nearly lunchtime back home, but after the adrenaline-charged day she'd just survived, Janey was a long way from feeling sleepy.

'Hold on guys,' Janey said, frowning. 'I think someone's at the door. Come in!'

'Freddy has something to say,' Celia said, tugging Freddy into the room.

Freddy's features twisted into a graceless scowl as four pairs of eyes scanned her with distaste.

'So *you're* Freddy,' Ness said, as she loomed forward into

the screen to see better. Ness, being Ness, had momentarily done something to Gabs's webcam and she had trouble seeing what was going on at Janey's end.

'Fellini huh?' Em added from the background. 'Couldn't you have picked some other cultural icon to trash in your quest to hound Janey out of Rome?'

'You're not as pretty as Janey's description of you,' said Gabs.

It was difficult for Janey to keep a straight face.

'I'm *not* apologising in front of *them*,' Freddy hissed at her mother.

'I don't see why not,' Janey replied, trying not to look like she was enjoying Freddy's discomfiture. 'They know all about it. I've told them every last sordid detail. They're really quite fascinated by what you managed to achieve in such a short space of time. You really had me going there.'

'You weren't exactly hard to track down on MySpace.' Freddy tossed her head. 'There aren't that many Janey Gs around. As soon as Mum told me of your *existence*, I found you just like that.' Freddy snapped her fingers.

'Clever you,' interrupted Em from the computer screen. 'Lucky Janes is such a nice person or you'd find the abject apology *you are about to give* all over YouTube.'

Celia had been listening to the rapid-fire exchange between the five girls with barely concealed amusement. 'Get on with it.' She gave her daughter a prod.

'I'm *sorry*,' Freddy spat. 'There, I'm done.' She turned on her heel and walked out, her 'international' hair swinging in her wake.

'And she really is, because I've grounded her until the end of the holidays, plus she has a new weekday curfew once school starts again. And I'm really sorry, too, Janey. Freddy's behaved monstrously with you because I turned a blind eye to her tantrums and her bad behaviour. The whole situation with her and her father is much, *much* harder work than my actual day job, and I've been taking refuge at the office. I guess I'd hoped that Freddy would work through the reasons for our divorce over time, but obviously I was wrong.' Celia shook her head. 'So *I'll* be spending more time at home as well, even if it means working after she goes to bed. You're going to be seeing an awful lot of both of us for the rest of your stay. Try and get some sleep soon? You've had a *very* trying day.' She closed the door behind her.

'You can say that again!' Janey exclaimed, turning back to the screen and her friends' smiling faces.

'You've had a *very* trying day,' Gabs repeated gravely.

All four girls fell about laughing, laughing even harder when Ness complained that she couldn't see anything because the camera wasn't working properly now *at all*.

It was almost noon when Janey woke on her second Friday in Rome, feeling somehow . . . lighter.

It seemed almost unreal that she would never be troubled by Fellini again – 'he' had been such a malevolent presence in her life for so many action-packed days!

Unexpectedly, both Celia and Freddy were still home and snoring in their respective beds. Janey figured they must've had the mother (and daughter!) of all talks last night and talked themselves out. Grabbing her backpack, Janey headed out and wandered the streets happily, just like any normal tourist, for the entire afternoon.

It felt good to be alive. Life was wonderful again, and Janey couldn't stop smiling. Later that afternoon, she returned with a peace offering – a tray of sweet ricotta cannoli.

'Mmmmmm,' Celia said, still in her dressing gown, as they shared them over coffee. 'My favourite!'

'That's exactly what the baker said,' Janey laughed. She'd purchased them at the pasticceria around the corner from Celia's building, and everyone there knew of the Australian woman who looked just like Janey.

Freddy deigned to pick at one as she sat listlessly at the kitchen bench. Her grounding had already started, and it was clear from her expression that the last week of her holidays now stretched long and pointlessly before her.

'I'll make dinner,' Celia said. 'Some comfort food would be just the thing. Pasta al forno, I think.' She set out the ingredients and put a pot of water on the stove to boil. 'We've agreed,' she added as she chopped onions, celery and fennel for the waiting pan, 'that *I'm* going to pull back a little with regard to work while *she's* going to employ a little less attitude around the place. Maybe next year I'll seek out a quieter diplomatic posting. Freddy's decided she doesn't need to live like Luz after all, and that she can afford to make new friends. Isn't that right, Freddy?'

Freddy glared at her. 'I was getting sick of them anyway,' she muttered, swallowing the last of her coffee. 'They're a bunch of try-hards, and Paolo has a drinking problem. We could always move to Paris,' she said, brightening. 'It's not that far from Rome, so I can see Papa, and the fashions are *primo*.'

'I was thinking more along the lines of Canberra,' Celia replied, whisking together a saucepan of béchamel sauce. A heavenly aroma filled the kitchen as she crumbled Italian sausage and minced veal into the frying pan. 'It'd be great for you to be back in Australia for Year 12.'

Freddy's face fell comically and Janey had to turn and pretend she was busy at the sink to stop a giggle escaping.

'But I'm open to negotiation,' Celia added mildly. She alternated layers of cooked meat and vegetables with cooked pasta and béchamel sauce in a large earthenware baking dish, topping off her creation with fresh breadcrumbs and shaved parmesan. 'Pass me the pepper grinder, would you?' she said to Janey with a wink.

It was going to be all right after all, Janey thought with relief, pushing the pepper grinder across the table to the aunt who looked so much like her, it was *spooky*.

Janey woke to *the most* amazing sight.

'Surprise!' Ness squealed as she, Em and Gabs plonked themselves down on the edge of Janey's bed. They each looked crumpled, but insanely wonderful to Janey.

She rubbed her eyes. The crumpled visions remained. What's more, Em sat on one of Janey's feet to prove she was really there. 'Sorry!' Em grinned, not sounding sorry at all.

'Are you dreaming?' Gabs added.

'Uh, I dunno!' Janey murmured, feeling light-headed. 'I might be! *OMG*!! What are you guys *doing* here?!'

The four of them squealed in unison, and Janey's three best friends in the world piled onto her bed and gave her the fiercest group hug of her life.

'Celia flew us in!' Em explained. 'She arranged it all yesterday through someone at the Rome embassy. To make up for Freddy's behaviour, she said. And hers. We basically had two hours to get our behinds to the airport and we were away. Someone from DFAT met us with tickets, paid for by your aunt.'

'Libby probably organised everything,' said Janey gratefully, remembering the Ambassador's efficient assistant. 'Go on!'

'And Celia kept it secret from everybody, even the beauteous Freddy,' said Em. ''Cause you know how snoopy Freddy is! She probably would've let the secret out early just to annoy you and her mum.'

Janey did some sluggish mental calculations. 'Um, doesn't that mean you've been flying *all night* to get here?'

'You bet,' said Gabs, a little wearily. 'Melbourne, Sydney, Honkers, London, Roma.' She rolled her 'r' at full volume like a crazed opera singer, making them all break out into fresh giggles. 'Non-stop all the way to get here to find you still doing a sleeping beauty at nine o'clock! What gives?'

'I'm on holidays,' Janey mock-complained, covering her

face with the doona. 'Give me a break.'

She threw the doona off a few seconds later. '*Spill*. Celia said it was the three of you who figured out what was going on.'

'Well,' said Gabs, 'Ness might be totally clueless about technology, but she's pretty sharp about *people*.'

'Um, thanks, I think,' said Ness, screwing up her face.

Gabs continued, 'And something about Fellini really bothered her as she reread all the stuff on your MySpace after we last talked to you. Something suddenly seemed to click...'

Em took up the story. 'So Inspector Ness, here,' Ness punched Em in the arm, 'tried to call me, but I'd just headed off to the scriptwriting thing – which was sensational by the way. So she dialled Gabs's place. And Gabs answered the phone sounding, uh, kinda weird.'

Janey raised her eyebrows. Gabs grimaced. 'I'd just done a ninety-minute bikram yoga session with Mum in a room heated to forty-point-five degrees Celsius. I'm so *not* cut out for exercise—'

'Especially not twenty-six asanas and, um, what were they called?' Em ribbed Gabs, 'Pranayamas? Pyjamaramas?'

Gabs giggled, then her tone turned serious. 'So Ness says, "Don't you think there's something screwy about this Fellini character who's been trashing Janey's profile?"'

Ness took over. 'In my vast retail experience, Janey, and you know it's vast—Everybody laughed. It was *so* true. 'Anyway,' Ness continued, 'I deal with insecure teen queens all day and I hear the way they speak about each other and their friends, or in some cases, like I said the other day, their *anti*-friends, and—'

'This is the best bit,' Gabs interrupted. 'Ness is totally the reason Luca came charging in like a white knight when Freddy and her henchpersons were playing out a scene from *Eyes Wide Shut*.'

Em snorted.

'I told Gabs that I didn't think Fellini was a guy at all!' said Ness triumphantly.

'I totally disagreed,' Gabs added. 'The creepy pic, the name, the weird profile, the whole stalking thing. That's such a loser *guy* thing to do! What girl has the time? So I demanded to know *why*.'

Ness grinned. 'And I pointed out how "he" was always so fixated on your *appearance*. Chicken head is like, slang for ugly girl, right? No guy ever writes like that. Well, none I know of, anyway.'

'But then we wondered what Brandon's involvement was because the links to Luca were too obvious and too clumsy,' Gabs continued. 'Brandon seemed pretty sweet on you. Remember the Café de Paris outing? And lunch at the Hotel Hassler? It just didn't add up.'

'Which is when we had the Eureka brainwave moment,' said Ness. 'Figuring that he had to be friends with the *real* person who wanted you gone!'

Janey clapped her hands together. 'So you worked out that Freddy was the connection!'

'It totally explained how Brandon was always right *there*,'

Gabs explained. 'And all those mixed messages he kept giving you. He's been simultaneously spying on you and falling for you.'

Ness took up the story. 'Of course he'd always be handy. *And* super conflicted. He's been following you around doing Freddy's dirty work but his heart probably hasn't been in it.'

'So Ness got in touch with Celia ASAP,' said Gabs. 'Outlining our theory.'

'I cut and pasted bits out of your MySpace so that Celia wouldn't think we were out of our minds,' said Ness. 'She needed proof of what we were saying. I mean, no one wants to hear stuff like this about their own kid . . .'

Gabs added, 'And we got in contact with Celia via the embassy's official email address because her personal one wasn't on the web.'

'But the stroke of genius,' said Em with a yawn, 'was that Gabs and Ness made sure that in no way did they alert Fellini, or you, to what they were doing. And that meant not commenting on your MySpace, Janes, until we were sure that Freddy really was behind things.'

'You're way too nice,' added Em. 'Unless we laid it all out for you, we knew you wouldn't want to believe that a long-lost family member was actually *doing* this to you.'

'You *can* be a bit of a sap,' Gabs agreed, as Janey pushed her right off the bed in mock outrage.

'Right.' Ness pulled the doona off Janey completely. 'Strategy needed. We have to hit Prada, Valentino, Fendi, Armani, Gucci and Missoni before lunchtime or I will *die*. I haven't been able to shop for about twenty-six hours because the others wouldn't let me go anywhere near the stores in any of the airports we had to run through to get here. Call a taxi! Now!'

Her friends laughed.

'Or better still, bring Luca back,' Em sighed. 'Now there's a hunk of spunk right there!'

'Didn't I say he was a dreamboat?' said Janey.

'Words failed me,' said Gabs in disbelief, because words never failed her, 'when we stumbled out of that sorry excuse for a baggage collection area and saw him standing there—'

Janey giggled.

'The sun gilding his curling dark hair and magnificent shoulders...' said Ness. 'Bouncing off his impeccably styled shades – Prada current season...'

'And holding a sign with our names on it!' Em squealed.

Janey's friends sighed in unison.

'And he was *so* easy to talk to,' said Gabs.

'Gabs sat in front,' said Ness enviously. 'Em and I were bobbing up and down like gophers in the back trying to get a word in edgeways, even a skerrick of his attention—'

'Basically, you hogged him,' Em said to Gabs accusingly.

'See? *See?*' Janey laughed as her friends pouted at each other. 'I wasn't exaggerating! He's divine.'

Through the half-open door to Janey's room they heard a derisive snort as Freddy turned on her heel and retreated down the hall. She'd been eavesdropping the whole time.

'She's just jealous,' said Em. 'You should've seen her

gobsmacked, classically beautiful features when we fell through the door this morning with Luca on our heels carrying our bags, and Celia welcoming us with open arms. Words cannot express how *delicious* it was.'

'It was karma,' said Ness simply.

'What goes around . . . comes around!' Janey giggled, recalling Brandon's mobile ringtone.

'Now get *up*, lazybones,' said Ness. 'The only thing that will fix my incredible jetlag is at least one pair of couture size 40 peep toes. And apparently, Romans are blessed with naturally *small* feet. So there should be plenty about.'

Gabs and Em rolled their eyes.

'The only thing that will fix me is *food*,' Em said plaintively.

'A big, aromatic bowl of pasta,' Gabs declared. 'With a chaser of semifreddo and a cappuccino on the side.'

'How's this for a strategy?' said Janey as she bounced out of bed and threw on some clothes. 'We grab a coffee at a shabby chic café I've been haunting just around the corner from here, then strip mine the designer stores around the Via Condotti for the rest of the day. Sound like a plan?'

The four girls grabbed their daypacks, sunnies and lipgloss, and squeezed through the door as one.

The last few days of Janey's holiday were the most memorable and fun-filled of her life so far.

The four girls stormed the boutiques like a horde of

conquering Vikings. They revisited Janey's favourite spots together, from Trastevere right through to the top of the Janiculum Hill. They dropped in on Gabriel Sansovino – the antique seller who'd sold Janey her keepsake painting of Rome – with an impromptu morning tea. He promptly returned the favour by treating them to lunch at Dal Bolognese, which overlooked the glorious Piazza del Popolo – the magical square depicted in the very oil painting that Janey had purchased from him.

And they even revisited the bone-filled chambers beneath the Santa Maria della Concezione church at the foot of the Via Veneto – which wasn't quite so creepy an experience with all of them there – and indulged Em's wish to gorge on tiramisù at the Café de Paris.

Janey introduced them to Luca properly when she and her best friends all joined him, his sister and their friends for the promised daytrip to the black sand beaches of Ostia. A trip that was the source of much laughter, teasing and goofy photography. Janey got horribly sunburnt but somehow it didn't matter, because late in the afternoon, Luca swam out with her to a floating pontoon moored far out in the ruffling water and asked whether he could come out to Australia to see her, later in the year. They sat and talked for a long time on the bobbing pontoon while the others looked on from the beach and gave them both space just to *be* with each other for a while.

This thing between them, whatever it was, thought Janey as they all piled tiredly back onto the train at the end of the day, might actually, maybe, one day, turn into *something*. Twenty-one and sixteen wouldn't be so very far apart, down the road. After the day they'd spent together getting to know each other's family – because if Janey was certain of one thing, her BFFs *were* her family as much as Celia and Freddy would ever be – Luca *felt* right. She wanted him in her life, and if it had to be via Skype, MySpace, email or carrier pigeon, so be it.

As if he heard her private thoughts, Luca turned his dark eyes upon her from the other side of the train carriage and smiled his heartbreaking smile.

'You're back,' sniped Freddy as Janey passed her in the hallway, her arms full of cushions. Janey was on her way to the living room, where her friends were camped out on mattresses.

Janey studied the younger girl, who looked even younger than she usually did because she had no make-up on and her hair wasn't styled to within an inch of its life. *Being grounded agrees with her*, Janey thought with an inner grin.

'Bored, were you?' said Janey, not unkindly.

'Me?' Freddy snorted. 'You wish!' She made to walk off, but turned abruptly. 'I wish I had *real* friends like yours. No one bothered updating me on MySpace today, even though I was online for hours just *waiting*.'

Janey's gaze softened. Yes, Freddy had been a horror head and caused her more anguish than she ever wished to experience again but she probably *was* lonely and bored and it *was* the school holidays.

'I'll speak to your mum and see what I can do,' Janey said.

Surprised, Freddy regarded Janey gratefully. 'I really am sorry,' she replied. 'It just got out of hand. I forgot you were a real person with real feelings. It really annoyed me how much Mum was looking forward to meeting you. She even left work early to take you out to dinner! She hardly ever does that with me. She just sends me over to Dad's.'

Janey grinned. 'Thanks to you, I'm seriously considering getting rid of my MySpace and starting a Facebook page!' She trailed off with a giggle, hearing an answering giggle behind her.

They had so much luggage that Celia had to organise a second embassy car to take all of them to the airport.

'Thanks for talking to Mum,' Freddy murmured to Janey as her friends took last-minute photos with Luca, promising to email him. 'If I hadn't had you guys to hang out with this week, I would've gone seriously stir-crazy. Your friends are great.'

'They are, aren't they?' Janey smiled. She gave Freddy a swift hug. '*You*, however, were a royal pain in the bum – but we're all good now, aren't we?'

Freddy nodded. 'If it'd been *you* doing it to *me*,' she said, 'I wouldn't have coped well *at all*.'

'Never would've happened,' Janey laughed. ''Cause I'm

nowhere near as devious as you are!'

'Are you sure you won't put Brandon out of his misery and at least call him before you leave?' Freddy added.

Janey looked thoughtful. Brandon had called her mobile several times over the last couple of days, but she'd passed on rehashing the whole Fellini misadventure. It turned out that the mystery Italian-speaking male who'd been sending Janey the creepy texts had been Paolo, but it still didn't excuse Brandon's involvement. Especially if he really did like her.

Janey shrugged. 'He knows where to find me – if he really *does* want to get to know me better he can write to me first and we'll see what happens. And tell him to use his own name this time! And definitely *no* creepy stuff.' Janey hugged Freddy again and told her, fiercely, to write.

Luca disengaged himself from Ness, Gabs and Em, and wandered over to where Janey was standing. 'You promise you'll come and see me?' she said to him, trying to sound cool. She wasn't sure of the right tone to project in a situation like this.

Luca nodded and took her hands in his. 'And I will email you and you will do the same for me, yes?'

Janey nodded, hoping she wouldn't cry when she had to walk away from him. 'It's been . . .' She struggled to find the words. So much had happened since she'd first met Luca outside this very building.

'You will take care of her?' Luca said with concern to Janey's friends, ranged protectively behind her.

'We will,' Gabs nodded.

Smiling through her sudden tears, Janey pulled her hands gently from Luca's and turned to face her aunt.

'We started out pretty rockily,' Celia said wryly, 'but the truth won out, hmm?'

She glanced over at Luca standing a little distance away, his dark eyes shielded by the shades he'd just put on. 'I've been wrong about so many things!' Celia whispered for Janey's benefit alone. 'At least *think* about what you want to do, and who you want to be with, can you promise me that?'

Janey nodded and gave her aunt a swift hug, too. 'I-it's really important to me that there's no more misunderstandings. About *anything*,' she said huskily.

Celia nodded. 'You, uh, wouldn't consider coming to live with us permanently would you?'

Janey felt as stunned at the surprise offer as her three best friends looked. She wondered if their shock was mirrored on her face.

'Hear me out!' Celia urged. From the corner of her eye, Janey registered Freddy's frozen expression of surprise at Celia's bombshell. 'You don't need to get on that plane. You could stay on with Freddy and me . . . I'm pretty confident now that meeting the terms of that stupid will wouldn't be a problem! You could finish your schooling here, Janey.'

Janey and her best friends exchanged glances. She could tell they were happy for her, but terrified at the same time that she might actually say *yes*! Gabs was practically holding her breath and turning purple.

For a crazy moment, Janey wondered what it would be like

to just walk away from her old life, right here and now.

Finally, she shook her head. 'Thanks again, Aunt Celia. But I'd like to finish school with my friends and all the things I know around me before I take up your offer. Even though I've loved my time with you in Rome . . . and I'm pretty confident now that Freddy and I can happily co-exist!' Janey and Celia shared a conspiratorial grin, 'I really just want to get back for now, and be with the people I love and see if I can stand on my own two feet and make a life for myself without anyone else's help.'

Celia nodded. 'I understand. Though I can't promise Freddy and I will still be based in Rome when you decide to come back to us.'

Celia hugged Janey tightly. Em, Gabs and Ness descended on Janey and linked their arms through hers before the four girls waved their final goodbyes to Luca, Celia and Freddy and swept through the departure gate together.

'What was the best bit about it all, do you think?' said Em as they lined up to board their plane.

'The food,' sighed Gabs.

'The accessories,' said Ness, who'd almost been slapped with extra duty on her back-breakingly heavy luggage until she managed to charm the ticketing officer into making an exception. Just this once.

The three of them looked over at Janey. 'All of it,' she declared mistily. 'It's just like Libby told Celia. It's *Rome*. It's practically spelt the same way as *romance*.'

She hugged the possibility of her brilliant future to herself and gave her friends an enormous smile. 'But for now,' she said, 'let's go home.'

About the Author

Rebecca Lim is an award-winning Australian writer, illustrator and editor and the author of over twenty books, including *Tiger Daughter* (a Victorian Premier's Literary Award-winner), *The Astrologer's Daughter* (A Kirkus Best Book and CBCA Notable Book) and the bestselling *Mercy*. Her work has been shortlisted for the Prime Minister's Literary Awards, NSW Premier's Literary Awards, Queensland Literary Awards, CBCA Book of the Year Awards and Foreword INDIES Book of the Year Awards, shortlisted multiple times for the Aurealis Awards and Davitt Awards, and longlisted for the Gold Inky Award, Margaret and Colin Roderick Literary Award, and the David Gemmell Legend Award. Her novels have been translated into German, French, Turkish, Portuguese, Polish and Russian. She is a co-founder of the Voices from the Intersection initiative and co-editor of *Meet Me at the Intersection*, a groundbreaking anthology of YA #OwnVoice memoir, poetry and fiction.

Mercy 'wakes' on a school bus bound for Paradise, a small town where everyone knows everyone else's business — or thinks they do. But they will never guess the secret Mercy is hiding ...

As an angel exiled from heaven and doomed to return repeatedly to Earth, Mercy is never sure whose life and body she will share each time. And her mind is filled with the desperate pleas of her beloved, Luc, who can only approach her in her dreams.

In Paradise, Mercy meets Ryan, whose sister was kidnapped two years ago and is now presumed dead. When another girl disappears, Mercy and Ryan know they must act before time runs out. But a host of angels are out for Mercy's blood and they won't rest until they find her and punish her — for a crime she doesn't remember committing ...

An electric combination of angels, mystery and romance, *Mercy* is the first book in a major new series.

www.ingramcontent.com/pod-product-compliance
Lightning Source LLC
LaVergne TN
LVHW041632060526
838200LV00040B/1550